RUNNERS

ALSO BY DAVID DELEE

RUNNERS

A Collection

DAVID DELEE

COPYRIGHT

ISBN: 978-1-962241-06-9

THIRD EDITION

For more information about new releases, special events, and exclusive content only available to subscribers, sign up to get David DeLee's newsletter

https://www.subscribepage.com/daviddelee

Thank you for purchasing this book. We hope you enjoy it.

CONTENTS

FIRST IMPRESSIONS

"WE DON'T GET a lot of folks like you up here."

Patrol Sergeant Sean Ritter sat behind a scarred desk stuffed into a cramped office in what served as a police station in the foothills of the White Mountains of New Hampshire. He leaned back in a creaky wooden chair that had seen better days and put his legs up over the corner of the desk, crossed them at the ankles. He wore salt-stained brown hiking boots with his forest-green uniform and dug dirt from under his fingernails with the blade of a small pocket knife.

"Latinas?" I asked with one raised eyebrow. While I'm only half-Latina—the other half is Irish—I do have dusky skin, raven black hair, and eyes as green as emerald pools. So, I've been told.

"Bounty hunters, Ms. deHaviland. We don't get many bounty hunters up here."

Oh. I'm quick to jump to conclusions too.

"So tell me. It's Grace, right? What brings a big city bounty hunter like yourself all the way out here to our little neck of the woods?"

I don't think of my home turf of Columbus, Ohio, as the big city, but if you police a community of six thousand people like Ritter does—I'd looked it up—I could see why he might think so. I put my PI license, my Bail Enforcement Agent ID, and a file folder on his desk.

The file contained the bail papers for Colin James Maynard, my legal authorization to pick him up.

"Colin Maynard's on trial for aggravated assault, battery, drug possession with intent to distribute, and child endangerment. Two days ago, the defense rested. The jury went to deliberate, and Colin jumped bail. New Hampshire law requires I check in with local law enforcement before I extricate. Consider me checked in."

Figuring my work here was done, I pocketed my credentials and reached for the file, but Ritter grabbed them. Damn it. I guessed I wasn't going to get away that easily. Ritter opened the file and flipped through the papers, slowly examining each document, one at a time. He grunted when he came to Maynard's mug shot.

When he reached the last page, he tossed the file back on the desk and returned to cleaning his fingernails. "And you think he's here?"

"I know he is."

I took back the file before he could grab it again. My wool-lined leather coat, stiff from the cold, crinkled with the movement. Late March, it's below freezing out here in the boonies, and there's still three feet of snow on the ground. At least in Columbus, there were some signs of spring by now; temperatures north of freezing, a few buds on the trees, oh, and no more snow.

"I found his car, an old '72 Charger," I added. "Still has the Ohio plates. It's parked outside an old rundown Cape on the outskirts of town." I gave Ritter the address.

His attention remained on his fingers. The nails were cut short, clean and neat. I put Ritter in his mid-to-late thirties. No wedding band. When he finished scrapping his fingers, he folded the little knife with a snap and put it in the pocket of his pants. He glanced up at me with pale blue eyes, the kind Huskies' have. On the thin side, he appeared to be in good shape. Someone who stayed fit through an active lifestyle, not a health club membership. A looker, too, I thought.

"How'd you happen to find his car at that particular house?"

Cranky about wasting time, I said, "You are familiar with the concept of police work, aren't you?" Ok, that came out a little bitchy, I supposed.

Ritter must have thought so, too, because he snapped up out of his chair so fast I took a step back. Not in fear but in defiance, setting my stance, fisting my hands.

His hands were clenched tight too. He leaned over the desk. "Now, you listen to me. I won't take being insulted by some smart-aleck bounty hunter. You wanna do that? You can just take your pretty little ass right on out of here and go back to Columbus, O-HI-O."

Did he just call me pretty?

I don't know if it was because I was tired since I'd driven for fourteen hours that day, straight in from Ohio, or if my Latin-Irish temper was just spoiling for a fight. Either way, I should have apologized—but I didn't.

Instead, I got into his face. "Fine with me. The only reason I'm here talking to you is because I have to. I found his car at that house because that's what I do. It's my job. And I'm damn good at it."

He stared at me long and hard. I stared back at him until it felt like all the air had been sucked out of the room. The overhead fluorescents buzzed like angry bees. The clock on the wall ticked off the minutes. Slowly and loudly.

If Ritter expected me to back down from his outburst, I didn't. If he thought I'd be intimidated by his authority, I wasn't. I'd been a cop, and I've dealt with cops my whole adult life. If Sean Ritter thought he could scare me, he was mistaken.

"Fair enough," he said, relaxing, settling back into his chair. Was he smiling? "Tell me about this Colin Maynard."

I didn't need or want anything from Ritter other than to inform him of my intentions to take Maynard, but I didn't want to make an enemy of him, either. I forced myself to relax as well.

"Maynard's a low-life junkie with a rap sheet a mile long. He's here because his girlfriend is here."

"This girlfriend got a name?"

"Allison Raynor. She's here with their son, Jimmy."

"I know most of the families around these parts—don't recognize the name." Ritter frowned. "That house you're talking about, I do know. It's abandoned. Been that way for years."

"I know," I said. "The owner of record is Gail Ackerman. I did a real property search."

Ritter nodded, seemingly impressed by my diligence. "Gail lived out there all her life. Died a few years back, just shy of her one-hundredth birthday."

"And without a will. The house is in probate." See police work. I tried not to look smug.

"This Maynard and his girlfriend, they're squatters." The gears were starting to click.

"Not exactly," I said. "Gail Ackerman had a sister—"

"Alyssa."

"How'd you…Oh, right. Small town."

He smiled.

I had to admit, it was growing on me.

"Alyssa was Allison's grandmother."

"That can't be right," Ritter countered. "Alyssa never married. She and Gail. They were a couple of old spinsters. Lived out at that old house all alone. Their whole lives."

"I can't speak to that," I said. "But Alyssa *did* get herself pregnant. In college, one year at OSU. She left the baby to be raised by the father. A jock from a local, well-to-do, but strict Catholic family. And the apple doesn't fall far from the tree. Twenty-two years ago, Alyssa's illegitimate daughter gave birth to Allison. Out of wedlock. No father is named on the birth certificate."

"You think this Allison Raynor's come here to lay claim to Gail's house?"

"I don't know. Don't care. I'm here for Colin Maynard. To bring him back to Ohio. The rest doesn't matter to me."

That put him off. "Well, aren't you the hard-ass?"

I get that a lot. "I know my job, Sergeant. I don't try and do anybody else's."

He took a minute. "So what's the deal with these two? They some kind of modern-day Bonnie and Clyde?"

"No. Just a couple of two-bit junkies. A few months back, the cops responded to a domestic disturbance call in the Short North section of Columbus. They arrived to find these two at each other's throats. The cops broke it up. Allison was beat to hell, and the apartment was full of drugs: cocaine, pills, crystal meth. The cops arrested them both and turned the whole thing over to the D.A.

"Allison cut a deal and agreed to testify against Maynard for the assault and drug possession. In exchange, she got a pass. Meanwhile, the idiot judge in his infinite wisdom—that's sarcasm, by the way."

Ritter nodded. "We've got that here, too."

"He let Colin Maynard out on bail. Ain't the legal system grand?"

"You sound bitter," he observed.

"Not at all," I said, not sounding very convincing. "I respect the legal system, just not the people running it. But hey, if they didn't keep letting these jokers out, I wouldn't have a job, so...."

"Maynard's not here to hook up. He's looking for payback."

"With these two, who knows? Maybe it's true love." I stopped before adding, I don't care. "My concern is getting Maynard and—"

He raised a hand. "You said. But this girl, her safety is *my* concern." Ritter came out from behind the desk. He stood at a lean six-foot-two. His uniform was expertly tailored with crisp, razor-sharp creases. He was squared away, except for those ugly, brown hiking boots. I pegged him as ex-military. "If she's in danger...."

"She won't be once I collar Maynard." I needed to get out of there before Ritter got any big ideas. "Now. Since I've complied with my legal obligation, Sergeant, consider yourself notified. I'll be on my way."

"Not so fast," Ritter said. "I'm coming with you."

Damn it. That was exactly what I didn't want to happen. "You don't have to. Really. I've got this." The last thing I needed was a tag-along.

"This is my town, Ms. deHaviland. You want to take this guy...."

At the door already, he held it open for me. "I come along."

Well, shit.

RITTER INSISTED WE take his vehicle. A Jeep Grand Cherokee, brown and white, complete with police emblem, whip antenna, and the full light-and-siren package.

I protested, wanting to make an inconspicuous approach.

He said relax. "It's too damn dark out there this time of night. They won't see us until we're right on top of 'em."

Turned out he wasn't wrong.

The moon was little more than a crescent sliver in the sky, playing hide-and-seek with some slow-moving, grey-black clouds. Ritter drove following a winding ribbon of black pavement carved between snow banks as high as the Jeep's hood. The asphalt was wet with runoff. Our tires whished. I worried about black ice. Black skeletal branches bowed heavily with ice and snow, creaked and swayed on either side of us. They glowed silver-white in our headlights as we passed.

"You always work alone?" Ritter asked over the blowing of the heater fans that weren't producing much heat.

"Usually. I've got a cop friend who helps me sometimes. She's a deputy with the Sheriff's Department."

"Sounds dangerous. Doing this alone."

The back of the Jeep fishtailed a little, enough to make my heart skip a beat, but Ritter corrected the skid without outward concern.

"It works for me."

After a moment, he said, "People need people."

An hour together, and the guy decides he knows me?

I shrugged. "I have a pet."

"That's something."

"A monkey. He's all the people I need. Or want."

He looked at me, his face awash in green from the dashboard lights. It was a handsome face, but hard to read. I shifted the conversation away from my least favorite topic. Me. "Been a cop long?"

"Seven years. Army before that."

Military. I'd called it. "See any action?"

"What is it with you? Just 'cause I'm a cop in a small town, you think we don't do any real police work here? All we do is write speeding tickets and teach DARE to school kids?"

Pretty much, but I kept that thought to myself. "Just making conversation. Why are you getting all defensive?"

"I'm not defensive." We drove on in silence for several more miles.

After a while, Ritter broke the silence. "So tell me. How does one get into bounty hunting?"

I thought back over the eight years since I'd been booted off the Sheriff's Department. About the hundreds of people who took off. Who ran from their obligations. Who would've left their families, their friends, and other loved ones holding the bag. Leaving them to wonder and worry about what had become of them. At least, that's what would have happened if I hadn't been there to stop them. To bring them in to face up to their mistakes. To face the justice they deserved.

I also thought about my father. How he abandoned my mother and me when I was seven. Left us without a word. No different than every worthless bail jumper I'd ever tracked down.

"I got drawn into it. I didn't have a choice." I said.

"Like a calling?"

The road forked up ahead. Ritter eased to the right.

I shouted, "Look out!"

Our headlights caught three deer gracefully leaping over the snow banks from a copse of trees. They ran across the road only a few feet ahead of us. The high beams shimmered off their smooth, brown flanks. Ritter tapped the brakes and slowed. We watched them run off into the woods, their little white tails twitching as they went. Then they stopped and turned, watching us watch them. What a great postcard moment, I thought.

When they moved off, Ritter resumed driving. "You said the girl has a kid with her. Is the kid Maynard's?"

"Far as I know. The boy, Jimmy, he was at the apartment when the cops busted the two of them. They found him hiding in a closet. His knees to his chest. His arms wrapped around his legs. Figure he hid in there when Maynard and Allison started beating the hell out of each other."

"Jeez."

"Guess you don't get crap like that around here, huh?" I sucked in my breath, realizing how that sounded like another snide swipe at his quiet little community. I didn't mean it to. After seeing the deer and being around the quaint beauty of the little town, I thought how peaceful it must be to live in a place like this.

I braced for Ritter's defensive barrage, not wanting to fight again.

"We get our share," he said simply. "Six months back, I got a call to check out a farm up on the county line. Earl Jenkins' place. Earl's got a wife, two kids—a son and a daughter. Odd folks. Kept to themselves mostly. Home-schooled the children so they could work the farm. Anyway, I get this call about gunshots out that way. I figure it's some kids out plinking tin cans with a .22 or something. No big deal."

He stared ahead, a part of him back in the past, reliving that day. His gloved hands tightened around the wheel. In the dim green dashboard lights, I saw his Adam's apple bob as he spoke.

"It wasn't kids plucking cans," I said.

"No. The boy, Eric. He got a hold of his father's pistol. Earl used it to shoot at the coyotes, keep them away from his stock. Eric used the gun to put two bullets into Earl. Then he shot his mom and his little sister. She was just nine years old. After that, he took a machete to each of them. Hacked them up, gutted them, cut off their arms and legs. There was blood and guts strewn everywhere. An awful mess. Coming up on all that, I called for backup. Then I started searching the property and found Eric. He'd hanged himself off the hayloft winch.

Hanging there, just twisting in the wind. Rope creaking. His face and bare chest were smeared in blood and guts. No note. No reason. Nothing." His voice grew soft. "Worse damn thing I've ever seen. And that's after two tours in Iraq."

Humbly, I began to revise my thoughts on rural policing. Cops do what cops do, no matter where they are. And human beings, with their insane capacity to brutalize, aren't bound by geography. Metropolitan or rural, killers are killers.

Ritter slowed the cruiser, pulled to the shoulder, and came to a stop. He shut off the headlights. "There it is." He pointed up ahead into the darkness. The moon peeked from behind the cloud cover but offered little in the way of illumination. Ahead, ice-encrusted, gnarled tree branches gave way to a lumpy blanket of snow covering a clearing edged by a slush-hardened snow bank and a solitary black mailbox. The mailbox leaned at an angle, buried up to its little red flag.

To make up for my less-than-charitable thoughts regarding Ritter and rural policing in general, I said, "Thanks for bringing me back out." I know, lame, right?

Ritter shrugged. "No problem." He shut off the engine. We stepped out into the cold.

I shivered. I thought I'd come prepared for the cold. I had on long sleeve under-armor, a black turtle neck sweater, and a wool-lined leather coat. Okay, the tight True Religion jeans were for fashion. And impractical. But the Uggs? They were both fashionable *and* practical.

Still, I was damned cold.

"Come on," Ritter said.

Together, we walked along the road. Black, wet, and icy despite the County's efforts to sand. Our breaths fogged the air. Ritter held my elbow, guiding me. When we reached the edge of the woods, where the trees gave way to the cleared property buried under three feet of fresh snow, we stopped.

Against the blackness of the woods, I made out the dark angular shape of the house. A sagging roofline. It's broken clapboard siding. No lights glowed inside the house, but Maynard's Charger sat in the unplowed driveway where the snow was tamped down and rutted by tire tracks. A dusting of snow covered the car: it hadn't moved. Colin Maynard was still inside.

The surrounding quiet was both peaceful and eerie. A silence had settled around us, marred only by the creaking of gently swaying trees—their ice-sheathed limbs scrapping, one against the other—and the whistle of a cold breeze.

Ritter gave my arm a gentle tug.

"Look. I know you think I'm just some backwoods, hick cop in the rural nothingness. And I am. But I'm not, too. I'm an M.P. with the National Guard. I did two tours in Iraq. I'm Ranger trained with the Army and SWAT trained with the state police. I don't get to use those skills much around here and to tell you the truth, I'm thankful for that. But I've used them enough. I know what I'm doing."

I stomped my feet. I wanted to cup my hands and blow into them, but I didn't. I thought it would call attention to my lack of proper clothing. My unpreparedness. I should have said I was sorry for my attitude. I didn't do that either. I wanted to, but the words wouldn't come out. I don't do contrite well.

He said, "Forget it. Give me ten minutes to get around back, then make your approach." He started to climb over the plowed mound of snow, his heavy hiking boots crunching through a scrim of ice.

"Hey." He was giving me the leeway I wanted. I touched his arm. "Why are you playing it this way?"

His brow furrowed. "How else would I play it? I've got no reason to go in there. No probable cause, no reasonable suspicion. As far as I can tell, the only play here is yours."

"Then why are you here?"

"I told you before. If that girl is in trouble, if she needs help, that's *my* job." He flashed a smile. "Also, I'm curious to see how a big city bounty hunter operates. Thought an old hick cop like me might learn something new."

"Right," I scoffed, scooping my hair up and winding a ponytail holder around it, returning his smile. "I figured you were here to teach me a trick or two."

"There's always that possibility as well. The night is young. You armed?"

I'm licensed to carry concealed in Ohio. But gun laws between there and New Hampshire are not reciprocal. Carrying a gun here, that would be illegal. I had three on me. "You really want to know?" I asked.

"No. Be careful."

His concern was touching. "I will."

Ritter moved off but stopped again. "Hey. Maybe after all this is done…you and I could, you know, go out and get something to eat?"

Really? Was he asking me out on a date? At a time like this?

Before I could say yes, he slipped off and got swallowed up by the darkness.

THE SMALL, NEW England Cape had a central front door, painted blue, and two large picture windows on either side, but only three blue shutters, one of which hung by a single hinge. Scraggily hedges weighted down by snow fronted the house on either side of the cracked cement stoop. There was no storm door. Carefully, I tried the doorknob. Locked.

I clenched a penlight between my teeth, which kept them from chattering and worked the deadbolt. The simple pin-and-tumbler cylinder made raking the pins with a pick and tension wrench a piece of cake. If I could keep my fingers from going numb in the cold. I managed.

I pocketed the burglar tools and the penlight and drew my Colt .45 autoloader, hoping I wouldn't need to shoot anyone.

I checked the clock on my cell phone. Twelve minutes had passed since Ritter left to go around back.

Holding my breath, I stepped into the dark interior, moving directly into a wide living room. Nightlights were plugged into outlets around the room, illuminating the space with a pale dull hue. Old couches and overstuffed chairs were shoved in piles to the right. Their cushions were soiled, torn, and tossed in disarray. A broken wooden table lay on its side with a rolled-up carpet folded and leaned against it. Something in the house smelled like it had been left on the stove for too long. And might still be there.

Two open archways led to the back of the house. Urine and mildew smells assaulted my nostrils. I covered my nose with the back of my hand and held my breath—it didn't help. And why was it so damned hot inside?

In the haze, a shadowy figure rolled off one of the couches and suddenly popped to his feet like a crazed jack-in-the-box.

I brought the .45 up in a two-handed grip. "Freeze!"

He didn't.

He ran for the back of the house.

"Colin! I know who you are." That bought me a second of hesitation before he ducked into the next room, swallowed up by the darkness inside. "My name is Grace deHaviland," I called out. "I'm a bail enforcement agent. I'm here to take you back to Columbus."

"I ain't going back," he shouted from somewhere in the darkness.

"Yes, you are," I said with confidence.

I sidestepped toward the doorway, my .45 aimed at the blackness. I squinted, looking for any sign of movement. "The only question is how much trouble we're going to have making it happen."

"Get back!"

"I can't do that, Colin."

I heard noises upstairs. Hard, angry footsteps stormed across bare wooden floors. I was close enough to the doorway to get an overview of the layout inside—a staircase leading upstairs. A hallway to the back of the house. Two rooms off to the right, bedrooms maybe.

A voice shouted down from the staircase. Female. Raw and angry. "Colin! What the hell are you doing down there?"

In the darkness, I watched a scarecrow of a woman stomping down the stairs wearing nothing but panties and a soiled-gray cami-top. She was barefoot. Her dishwater blonde hair was a frizzy mess. She had a little boy in tow, his forehead furrowed as he wiped sleep from his eyes.

Allison Raynor and her son, Jimmy.

Colin shouted up the stairs. "Go back upstairs, Allie. I'm handling this."

"Handling what?" Seeing me, Allison narrowed her ghoulish eyes. Wide, bloodshot orbs surrounded by dark, baggy circles. Her face was gaunt, so thin and wasted away. It looked like a death mask. "Who the…"

The hand not clutching Jimmy's wrist came out from behind her leg. It held a gun. She squeezed off two rounds. I dove to the right, cursing as I knocked over a table and crashed into the rolled-up carpet. Sprawled on the dust-covered floor, I raised my gun, aiming it at the doorway and half expecting to get a bullet in the face. Instead, I heard Colin and Allison shouting. And footsteps. Running.

I scrambled to my feet, coughing from the moldy dust I'd stirred up. I charged toward the doorway. At the doorframe,

I crouched, swept the hallway. Clear. Were they hiding in the two rear bedrooms? No. I would have heard the doors slamming shut. Had they run upstairs? No. Those footsteps would have sounded different; I would have been able to tell, even over the pulse hammering inside my ears. Right?

I made my way toward the back of the house. Another doorway. I darted into a mudroom filled with coats and boots, mittens, and scarves. Here a door led out to the back. It was closed. Again no slamming doors, no blast of ice-cold air from outside. I moved directly into the kitchen. Empty.

A single bulb shone over the sink. Its weak light revealed a porcelain sink and cheap Formica countertops. A folding metal table filled the small kitchen space. On it were dishes, plastic bottles, bags of fertilizer, Pyrex beakers, a Bunsen burner—burning—rubber tubes, and under it all, a propane gas tank. The littered contents and the noxious fumes from the flaming Bunsen burner told me what I'd stumbled into.

A frigging meth lab.

The windows were boarded over with plywood, keeping out prying eyes.

I looped around the table and rushed through the empty dining room. I shimmied up to the far side of the large archway leading back into the living room. Across the room, I saw Colin and the boy. They'd reached the front door. Had it open, dropping the temperature in the house by ten degrees.

"Don't do it, Colin. Don't you run."

He leveled me with a hard stare, holding the boy tight. Jimmy stared at me too. Wide-eyed, looking scared in his Iron Man pajamas. Where the hell was Allison? She was the one I worried about. She was the one with the gun.

She didn't remain hidden for long. Having circled around, she came at me from behind, from the kitchen. I caught movement from the corner of my eye, her shadow in the doorway blocking the glow of the single kitchen light. It gleamed off the gun she held and aimed. A Browning 9mm.

The woman fired.

I dropped to one knee and brought up my gun. I supported it with my weak hand, lined up my shot.

Before I could fire, the rear door burst open. Allison spun. In quick succession, I heard two shots, and Allison scream. Her body fell back. With pin-wheeling arms, she crashed into the table. Its flimsy metal legs buckled and collapsed. Two red splotches soaked her soiled cami. Two well-placed shots. One in the gut. One over her right breast.

Ritter remained crouched at the back door. His arms locked in a two-handed grip. He stared with a steely intensity over the gunsights. Slow to straighten up.

I rushed to the doorway. Flames whooshed up from the table, now collapsed. The toppled burner had ignited a river of spilled liquids now pooling on the floor. The flames licked at Allison's body. In that little bit of time, the fire had already climbed several feet into the air.

Colin called out from the front door where he'd remained. "What's going on?"

Ritter moved toward the burning pyre. He tugged at Allison's blazing body, trying to pull her from the flames.

Shit. I moved closer. I had to raise my arm against the heat. It was too late for the woman.

"Ritter!"

Already the heat was intense enough to drive me back. I had to squint against the brightness of the fire, the toxic smoke. My eyes watered. My nose and throat burned. "It's too late!"

"No!" Ritter wiped sweat sheen from his brow. "Get out! The propane tank…it's gonna blow."

Crouched over Allison, he rolled her and patted at her burning clothes, trying to smother the flames. I rushed to the metal table, crushed and bent and mangled. I flipped it over to the sound of crashing tin plates and shattering glass. The flames whooshed up around it with an angry roar. I stomped down the table, smothering much of the fire underneath. Still, the spilled liquids, spreading, continued to burn. The flames raced quickly across the floor and climbed up the kitchen counters and walls, bubbling and peeling the old yellow paint. Flame engulfed the splattered propane tank.

I'm a city girl and don't know much about propane tanks, but even I knew having one in the middle of a bonfire was not good. As I tried to edge around the inferno, something grabbed my arm and pulled me back. Colin Maynard rushed past me, charging in from the dining room. He held two sofa cushions in his hands.

Using the cushions like oversized oven mitts, he scooped up the burning tank, coated in flaming liquid, and shouted at Ritter, "Open the door! Quick! Get out of the way!"

Ritter swung the back door open. Broken glass crunched under his feet. Colin ran at him with a wave of flames shooting off the tank. He pitched the flaming tank into the backyard, tossed the two burning cushions away, and shouted, "Get down!"

The back door slammed shut. We turned and hunched to the floor, waiting for the explosion. It didn't take long. The blast came with a resounding boom, followed by the sound of shredded metal pelting the back of the house and breaking windows.

In the silence that followed, I let out a breath. "Jesus."

HALF AN HOUR later, I stood in the road outside Gail Ackerson's house, now ablaze with generator-powered work lamps set up by the arriving volunteer firemen. They put down the fire quickly, soaking the back of the house and yard with water and foam to keep the old tinderbox from going entirely up in flames. Water, tuned to ice, hung from the roof's edges like icicle-tipped drapes. Ritter was out back with the state police, the county sheriff, and a couple of civilians. Town council types and attorneys from the prosecutor's office. Allison Raynor had been rushed to the hospital, alive but critical.

Colin Maynard stood beside Jimmy, who sat at the open back doors of an ambulance. The boy had a blanket draped over his thin shoulders while a pretty paramedic gently attended to the boy's scrapes, bumps, and bruises.

Sean Ritter came from behind the house, watching me watch Colin and Jimmy. Colin doted over the boy, mussing his stringy hair and demonstrating nauseating fatherly concern. Not acting at all like the Colin Maynard I'd read about in the bail file.

"A quarter for your thoughts," Ritter said.

I gave him a quizzical look. "A quarter?" I asked.

"You're in the Northeast. Everything's more expensive here." He jutted his chin out toward Colin. "What are you going to do about them?"

Maynard put an arm around Jimmy, and pulled him in close for a hug. A lump formed in my throat. Why had Maynard come back? Why had he saved our lives when he could have run? Been gone. Free and clear. And did it matter? It didn't change what I had to do.

"I don't know," I said.

Colin straightened up as we walked over. Jimmy stiffened. The boy looked up at his father, eyes wide. "Dad?"

"Sit tight, buddy. I need to talk to these officers."

"Okay, Dad." The boy looked down, sullen and worried. The paramedic offered him a lollipop. He brightened at that. "Cherry?"

"What happens now?" Colin asked me. "I go with you?"

"I've got a few questions first," Ritter said. He pulled a notepad from his back pocket and flipped it open to a clean page. "Tell me what you were doing here. Did you come here to hurt that girl for testifying against you?"

"What? Allison? No, I came here for Jimmy."

I glanced over at the ambulance. "For the boy? Why?"

Maynard paused to gather his thoughts. He was smart. He knew what he said and did next would have a profound effect on his future. "I mean… Look." He focused his attention right on me. "That shit back in Columbus. It was never about beating up Allie like the cops and the lawyers said. It was about me protecting Jimmy."

"Protecting him from what?"

"From Allie."

I hadn't seen that one coming. "Explain."

"Allie's a mess. When she's not out of her mind on drugs, she's out of her mind jonesing for her next hit. Jimmy's not safe with her. She'd go out and leave him alone, sometimes for days. No food. No way to take care of himself. She'd hit him if he got on her nerves, which was often. She even had him shoplifting for her. She'd use the stuff they stole to score more drugs."

Ritter interrupted. "So this meth lab here, it's not your set-up?"

"Hell no. I'm clean, man. One-hundred-eighty-seven days, not a pop." He whipped off the coat someone had given him to show us his arms. He had track marks. Lots of them. But they were old and scabbed over. "I was putting money aside, saving up so I could take Jimmy and get him away from her, away from Ohio."

"Why'd you beat her up?" I asked.

"I never touched her. Not ever. All that shit, when the cops got there, I was defending myself. From her. Listen. I went there to get Jimmy, to get him the hell away from her. I was ready to go, had money saved up, and everything. But, Allie. She was so strung out. She went crazy and attacked *me*. Demanded I give her the money for herself. I told her no. She went nuts. Started swinging at me, clawing at my face. I knocked her back. I admit it. I did, but only to defend myself. That's all. I swear."

"I saw the police photos," I said. "She looked like a punching bag."

"That was from her dealer. Stupid bitch was selling for some asshole. But she tried to hold out on him, kept product for herself. He found out. Look, we fought, yelling, screaming, and shit like that. All the time. It was bad. Always bad. But I never hit her. Never. Not even before I got myself clean. I swear. I tried to get her to dry out, too. Do rehab with me, but she refused."

"Let me get this straight," I said. "You jumped bail and came all this way. Just to get the boy?"

"That's right." He nodded. "They were gonna convict me. I'm looking at hard time. I can't go to jail and let her keep Jimmy. I just can't. Jimmy and me. We were all set to take off. We were gonna be gone."

I tried to read his expression in the pulsating blue emergency lights. He appeared genuine. Sincere. But I'd bought that t-shirt before—with bad results. "Why would she suddenly let Jimmy go now when she wouldn't before?"

Maynard looked over at his son. When he spoke, his voice broke. "Because I paid her. I gave her the money. Everything I have. Everything I've saved." He turned away so I couldn't see his face. Too late. I saw the tears in his eyes. "Imagine that," he said. "I had to buy my son from her."

When I was sure my voice wouldn't crack, I said, "Then what? You two have someplace to go?"

Excited, he nodded. "I got a job. It's through a friend of a friend. In New Brunswick."

"Canada?" Ritter asked.

"Yeah. On a fishing boat. Jimmy and me. We were heading to Canada. I was going to learn how to fish." Then he got quiet, realizing Canada wasn't in his future. Columbus, Ohio, was, and there, a long stint in prison.

A voice nagged at the back of my brain. It said: *Right and wrong aren't in your job description. You don't play judge and jury, and they don't track down bail jumpers.*

Ritter waved me away from Colin Maynard. Out of earshot, he asked, "What'd'ya think?"

"Make believe."

"I'm not so sure," Ritter said. He held up a hand to stop my protest. "But I'm not intervening. This is your play."

"You're saying I should cut Maynard loose?"

He shook his head. "I'm saying it's your call entirely. But before you decide, think about that little boy. His mother, if she survives, is going away for a very long time. If the dad goes away too? The kid, he's got no one."

He let that hang. I glanced over at Colin. He'd returned to the ambulance, to his boy. Jimmy hugged his father, pressed his face tight into his gut.

"He probably saved our lives," Ritter nudged. "And I don't know 'bout where you're from. Foster care … not where I'd like to see a kid brought up."

My call? Yeah, right. My dad ran out at me when I was about Jimmy's age. But I had my mom. I wondered where I'd have ended up without her. Hell, how I almost ended up, even with her. What chance would Jimmy have? with no one. Or worse, his mother.

"Shit." I stormed over to Colin. "This job in Canada, it's legit?"

"Absolutely. Look." Excited, Colin rooted around in his pants pocket. "Here's the letter I got."

I looked over the crumpled, folded paper he handed me. It was an acceptance letter. Complete with a start date on what looked like official company stationary. It had been opened and refolded many times. A tangible link to a new life. A fresh start. A way out.

After reading it, I slowly folded the paper along the worn lines. I handed it back to him. "Get out of here."

Open-mouthed, Colin said, "Really? You're serious?"

I nodded. "But you listen to me. It's illegal for me to cross international borders to go after a bail jumper."

He nodded, listening.

"I don't care. In fact, I've done it before. You mess this up. I'll do it again. Understand?"

He nodded vigorously. "Yes, ma'am. I hear."

"And don't come back to the States, not ever."

"I won't. Thank you." He looked to Ritter. "Both of you."

He and Jimmy ran for the Charger, excited and chatting. He fired up the car and backed out, threading through the emergency vehicles.

When the red taillights had disappeared, Ritter said, "You did the right thing."

"You know how much money that just cost me?" I asked.

He laughed. "For a big city bounty hunter, you're not such a hard-ass after all."

I put a finger to my lips. "Shush. You'll ruin my rep."

He smiled. I was really starting to like that smile.

"And for backwoods, hick cop from the boonies, you're not so bad yourself. Now. Didn't you say something earlier about getting something to eat?"

"I did."

"Good. And it's on you," I said with a smile of my own. "Since because of you, now I'm broke."

###

FUTILE EFFORT

THIS WAS THE part I hated. Talking to the families, trying to solicit information from them, to get them to tell me things, things that would put their loved ones back in jail. *For their own good*, I say, using every ounce of feminine charm I can muster to convince them.

In the west end of Columbus, a few blocks off Broad Street, the house was the size of a small cottage. Fronted by a postage stamp size yard, it had a little concrete stoop with a tin awning overhead. Black iron bars were welded over the windows. The gravel driveway was rutted from use and neglect.

I knocked on the wrought iron-covered storm door and waited.

A thickset woman in a plain blue housedress opened the door the width of a security chain. She had a dark, round face and black hair streaked with gray.

"Yes," she asked, her tone laced with suspicion.

I gave her my brightest smile. "Mrs. Lopez? My name is Grace deHaviland." I showed her my badge and private investigator's license. "I'm a bail enforcement agent. I'd like to ask you some questions about your son, Mateo."

"Matty's not here. Go away."

My left foot prevented her from slamming the door in my face. "I'm afraid I need to insist, Mrs. Lopez. Mateo missed his appointment in court yesterday. I've been hired to bring him in."

Her forehead creased and her eyes narrowed. She took a moment to decide what to do next. She looked down at my foot. "I need to unlock the chain."

Bounty hunters have the authority to enter a person's private property without a warrant or permission to effect a re-arrest. I nodded to Mrs. Lopez and removed my foot, hoping I wouldn't have to shoulder my way in.

She slammed the door, slipped the chain, and a second later, opened the door again.

I stepped inside, directly into the living room.

She shut the door behind me.

The room was small but neat, clean, and smelled faintly of furniture polish. Looking around, I took in the dozens of heavily framed pictures on the facing wall and the large, flat-screen TV on an old refinished steamer trunk off to one side.

A single window with side panels offered a little natural light, and a brass floor lamp with three spotlights provided the rest. Under the window were two club chairs with arm doilies and a linen-draped accent table between them. It was family photographs of every imaginable size and shape. I took a moment to look them over under Mrs. Lopez's watchful eye.

The majority of them were of Mateo Lopez: Mateo as a kid in a Little League uniform: a teenage Mateo sitting bare-chested in a lounge chair at the beach: Mateo behind the wheel of an orange muscle car, a broad grin on his face. I picked up one from when Mateo was a baby, held proudly by a young man with gang tattoos covering his arms.

"His father?" I asked.

Mrs. Lopez nodded. "He's gone."

She was in a number of the photos;, younger, thinner, prettier. Before life had taken its toll on her. In a few, a young girl with long dark hair and copper-colored skin, as pretty as her mother once had been, smiled brightly. She was probably fourteen or fifteen in the most recent one.

I picked it up. "Is this your daughter?"

"*Si.*"

"I didn't realize Mateo had a sister."

"Rosario. She doesn't live with us anymore."

Curt. Unwilling to cooperate. I get that a lot. Few people I interview like talking with me. "I know this is hard for you, Mrs. Lopez, but it's important I find Mateo. For his sake."

She picked up a photo of her son. In it, he appeared to be a few years younger than his current seventeen. He wore a baseball jersey and had on a Cincinnati Reds baseball cap. He was smiling. She ran her fingertips over the glass surface.

When she spoke, her chin trembled. "He is the good one." Tears welled in her eyes and then fell, tracking down her dusky cheeks. She brushed them away.

"You mean Mateo's never been in trouble before?" I had a copy of his arrest report with the bail papers. My authorization to apprehend him. This was his first arrest. Unfortunately, his initiation into a life of crime had started with a serious aggravated assault charge stemming from a fight with a young man outside a bar. Mateo beat the other man so badly he put him in the hospital.

"Never," Mrs. Lopez said about her boy. "He is a good boy. A good student. He works hard at school. And he has a part-time job," she added, trying to convince me of his virtues.

"Do you know where Mateo is now, Mrs. Lopez? Will he be coming back here?"

She took a long time before answering. "No. He left. He didn't say where. I told him he had to stay. To take responsibility for what he's done." Her gaze fell on the collection of framed pictures. "To no' be like his father. Or his sister."

"Does he have a cell phone? Can you call him?"

"No. He no have a phone." She shook her head. Disappointed. Angry. Ashamed. Maybe it was all three. And more. "I want him to do right'. I tell him stay. What is life on the run? I am afraid for him."

"I understand. That's why I'm here. Do you have any idea where he would go? Who he would go to for help? His sister, perhaps?"

"Rosario?" She shook her head again. "She is like her father, a waste. No help to him. I am sorry. A mother should no say these things about her daughter, but it is true. Drugs destroyed her. She is gone. I do not know where she is. Neither does Matty."

"Mrs. Lopez. The judge has issued a bench warrant for Mateo. Do you know what that means?"

She shot me an angry look. "Of course, I know. The police, they will arrest him. If they find him. Like you."

"No, Mrs. Lopez. Not like me. The police don't care about Mateo. Don't care if he gets hurt."

I needed to bring the kid in alive and in relatively one piece if I was to collect the bounty. That sounded hard-hearted, but I did care about the kid too. A first-time offender. It would be easy for him to react badly to a police confrontation, get himself hurt.

"And you do?" She waved a dismissive hand. "You are just trying to scare me."

That was true too, but I wasn't going to admit that. "What about his friends, Mrs. Lopez? Kids Mateo hangs out with? Is there anybody he would go to see? Anyone who would know where he is? Please tell me. I want to help."

"Why should I believe you?"

I thought about my teenage years. I was an angry kid. Rebellious and stupid. The trouble I'd caused my mother. The sleepless nights. The indignity she'd endured bailing me out of jail. Our endless fights. I couldn't dump my usual spiel on this woman, tell her how the cops don't care about Mateo. That they'd shoot him if he gave them any trouble. That I only got paid if I brought him in alive. Provoking a mother's fear is a great way to motivate someone to talk.

But seeing the pain in this woman's eyes, I couldn't do that to her. I couldn't add to what was clearly an already overwhelming burden that way.

"I got into a lot of trouble when I was Mateo's age," I told her. "I know it looks bad now. But it will only get worse if he continues down this path. If he doesn't come in. Please, help me help him."

She studied me for a long time. Then she asked, "You are Latina?"

I nodded. "On my mother's side. My father was Irish."

Again, Mrs. Lopez studied me, making up her mind. Finally, she nodded. "There is one boy. If anybody knows where my Matty is, Sketcher does."

THE SCHOOLYARD WHERE Mrs. Lopez told me I could find Sketcher was less than a mile from the Lopez home. As I drove away from her house, I tried to shake off the weight that had settled on me. But I couldn't.

Was the deteriorated neighborhood around me contributing to my black mood?

The tiny houses in such disrepair. The yards filled with junk. The rusted, loose fences. The broken sidewalks. The cars up on blocks. The brick walls tagged with spray-painted graffiti. Or maybe my depressive mood came from how much Mrs. Lopez reminded me of my mother. How hard being a single parent must be, struggling to raise kids in such an environment. For Mrs. Lopez, who'd had one head off the tracks so early and so completely. To have her second following fast down that same path. It must be heartbreaking.

I wondered if that was how Mom felt raising me.

I reached the school where several young men were on the basketball court. They weren't playing basketball, though: they were engaged in a rousing game of good-old stickball. An orange strike zone had been painted on the concrete wall separating the courts from the upper-level fields. A skinny Latino in low-riding khaki shorts, high-top sneakers, and no shirt stood in a batter's box spray painted on the court. He clutched a sawed-off broom handle in his hands.

Another young man, this one African-American, wound up and pitched a yellow tennis ball.

The swing.

A hollow popping sound and the tennis ball sailed high into the air. The boys in the outfield called for it and shuffled into position, their hands shading their eyes from the late afternoon sun. With a chorus of *I've got it, I got it*, the ball was caught. One away.

I ducked through the hole cut into the chain link fence.

Before the next batter came to the plate, I called out, "Hey, boys."

The pitcher turned with a wolf-like grin. "Hey, baby."

"Come to play," another one shouted.

"You can be on my team," the new batter said, tapping the broomstick on the "plate" a few times.

"Another time, thanks. I'm here for Sketcher."

A thin, wiry Latino playing the outfield snatched a hoodie off the ground and tugged it over his head and shoulders. He popped the hood up to cover his head. He looked like Eminem in *8 Mile*. Mrs. Lopez had described Mateo's friends as good kids. She said they hung out playing stickball rather than cruising, looking for trouble. They were good in school, she said. None were dropouts. They didn't hang around the pool hall and the street corner doing drugs like most of the kids from the neighborhood.

"What do you want?" Sketcher asked, "I haven't done anything."

"I didn't say you did. Can we talk?"

"Sketch don't wanna, I will, baby," the pitcher called out.

"I'll tell you everything, sweet thing," the batter said.

"Yo, why don't you be cool, huh?" Sketcher shook his head. "They're like little kids." He jogged over to me. When we were out of earshot of his friends, he said, "What do you want? Who are you?"

"My name is Grace deHaviland. I'm a bounty hunter."

That got his attention. "A bounty hunter. For real?"

"For real."

"This about Mateo, right?" He seemed genuinely concerned for his friend.

"Yes, I'm afraid it is. When was the last time you saw him?"

"What's gonna happen to him, I tell you?"

I decided to be honest with the kid. "It's my job to find him, to bring him back to court."

"You want me to rat?" He glanced over at his friends, who watched us intently.

"I want you to help him. I'm afraid he'll get hurt."

"You got that right." His eyes glinted in a way that told me I'd struck a chord.

"What do you mean by that?"

"He was here. 'Bout an hour ago."

"Where did he go?"

He shrugged. "Don't know."

My skepticism must have shone because Sketcher went from cooperative to defensive in a heartbeat. "Serious. I don't.

He came here wanting to know if anybody knew this dude named Dink."

"Who's that?"

"I don't know. I've never heard of 'im but Fat Jack...." He turned and pointed to a short, fat black kid sitting on the concrete in what would be left field, eating a Snickers bar. "He says the dude hangs out at the movie theater. Downtown."

"The one in the Arena District?"

"Yeah. That one."

"Why?"

"I don't know. He likes movies, I guess." He laughed at his own cleverness.

"Funny. I meant, what did Mateo want with this Dink?"

"A gun. Mateo went to find him to buy a gun."

I THREADED MY way downtown through late afternoon traffic. When I reached Nationwide Arena, I pulled into the parking structure across the street. The movie theater was a block away.

Searching for a parking space, I felt pumped, knowing I was only about an hour behind Mateo. But I couldn't shake this bad feeling I'd started to get. The gun thing bothered me. It didn't track with what I knew about Mateo Lopez. Here was a kid, seventeen years old, who'd managed up to this point to stay out of trouble despite growing up in a pretty rough part of town with a troubled sister and a father who'd abandoned him. Judging from the prison tats I saw in the photograph, that was probably the only good thing the father had done in his life.

Now, suddenly, Mateo was assaulting people outside of bars, jumping bail, and trying to get a gun. None of that made sense.

I found a spot, parked, and strolled through the parking structure, enjoying the shady, cool respite from the summer sun outside. I went over in my mind what I knew about Mateo's arrest. It had happened outside a sleazy dive in West Columbus, right on Broad Street. The cops had responded to an anonymous 911 call, probably from a neighbor disturbed by the noise. When they arrived, they found Mateo standing over his victim, having just beaten him senseless. His knuckles were bruised and bloody. They took Mateo into custody, but he refused to talk to the cops. The victim, a gang-banger in his late twenties named Ramon Santiago, was taken to the hospital in a coma.

Who was Ramon Santiago to Mateo? Why had Mateo fought with him? And why did the boy now want a gun?

Since it was late afternoon, only a few people were hanging around inside the theater lobby. A handful of kids milled around playing the arcades in the game room. I watched a father and his little girl as they talked excitedly, checking out a poster for the latest Pixar film. Holding hands, they walked into one of the several theaters in the multiplex. He was smiling, and she was laughing. They were happy.

My father never took me to a movie when I was a kid. Not that I recalled.

I showed Mateo's mug shot to the girl in the ticket booth and the three boys in ill-fitting red jackets throwing popcorn at each other behind the concession stand. No one had seen Mateo. At least, that's what they all told me.

Disappointed and not sure where to turn next, I started to leave. I stopped when I saw an elderly man wearing gray coveralls backing out of a utility closet carrying a broom and long-handled dustpan. He had short-cropped gray hair and thin, hunched shoulders. He moved around with a stooped gait but kept an eye on the lobby with surprisingly clear, sharp eyes.

I went over to talk to him. "Excuse me."

"Yes. Can I help you?" Polite but cautious.

I showed him Mateo's picture. "Have you seen this boy here today?"

He folded his hands over the top of his broom and dustpan. "Why you looking for him?"

"I'm a bail enforcement officer." I pulled out my badge and PI's license. "He skipped bail this morning. I'm trying to locate him."

"Bounty hunter, huh?"

"Yes, sir."

"Never met no bounty hunter before," he said with a playful smile. "Wouldn't have pictured they look like you."

I smiled back, appreciating the compliment. "Most of them don't, but thanks. The boy?"

"What? Oh, yeah, sure. I seen him. He was here a while, hanging around until he met up with the local trash. A punk named Dink."

My heart skipped a beat at hearing the name Dink. Sketcher hadn't steered me wrong. "They were here together?"

"Sure. Dink, he's around all the time. I chase his ass out of here more times a day than I can count. Punk ass. Hangs out playing the arcades. But I know what he's really up to."

"I understand he deals guns."

"Guns. Drugs. Stolen credit cards. Deals in all of it. I call the cops, but it don't do no good. They send him away, but he always comes back. That other boy? First time I've seen him here. What'd he do?"

"He beat up a guy. Put him in a coma. Now he's on the run."

"Why?" The elderly black man appeared interested.

"Why what?

"Why'd he beat the guy up?"

"Does it matter?"

"Might. Maybe he had a good reason for doing it."

And maybe he didn't, I thought. "I'll ask him when I find him. How long ago was he here?"

"Just. He met up with Dink, and they left. Couldn't of been more than ten, twenty minutes ago."

I enjoyed a sudden adrenaline surge. I was closing in. Talking fast, I said, "Do you have any idea which way they went? What they were doing? What they talked about?"

He held up his hand. "Slow down. Slow down. I don't know for sure, but I can guess where they are."

Surprised and delighted, I practically squealed. "You can?"

"Sure." He pointed out the doors to the left with a hand gnarled by arthritis. "Down that way to the end of the alley. There's a fenced-off area where the garbage containers are at. It's where Dink does all his business. The outside cameras, they don't cover that area. That good-for-nothing Dink knows it."

I thanked him and blasted through the door, out into the fading sunlight.

HEADING DOWN THE back alley, I drew my weapon, a Colt .45 semiautomatic. Most people are surprised I carry something that big. Girls are supposed to carry a little 9 mil or a Lady Smith, like my best friend, sheriff's deputy Suzie Jensen. Not me. I like to know that if I need to put someone down, they'll stay down. With my .45, they do.

The sun had started its descent, casting the walkway around the parking structure into deep shadow. I sidestepped along the sandstone and brick wall of the parking lot, choosing my way carefully, keeping as quiet as I could. At the corner, I heard voices. Too low for me to make out the words, but they told me where my runner was.

The voices came from around the corner where a wooden fence butted up to a low concrete dividing wall that separated the movie theater parking lot from a second, lower-level parking structure below. I trotted silently to the enclosure, then stepped around the fence, bringing my gun up in a two-handed grip, about to yell *freeze* or something equally clichéd.

Instead, I ducked, a move that saved me from getting my head caved in by a wooden board swung at me like a club by a little shrimp of a kid. Guess I wasn't as stealthy as I thought. The board smacked into the fence with a loud, reverberating crack.

"Hey!" I shouted.

At barely five-foot-two, Dink lived up to his name. He dropped the board and hopped over the short half-wall, and disappeared. I reached the wall in time to see him hit the concrete ramp leading to the underground portion of the next garage. The drop was only about eight or nine feet down. I could have made the jump if I'd wanted to. Really. I could have.

But Dink wasn't the one I had paper on. I spun around. Mateo Lopez was hoofing it fast across the street and through an adjacent surface parking lot. I holstered my gun and took off after him.

He zigzagged through the rows of cars like a wide receiver charging out of the backfield. He was fast. But so was I. Rather than chase after him by following his serpentine path, I ran in a straight line, hopping onto the hood of the first car I came to. A Lexus. I ran over the hood and jumped to the trunk of the next car in line, then down to the ground. I did that again over the next line of cars, and the next, trying not to think about the damage my boots might be doing to the hoods and roofs and trunks I was trampling.

Mateo and I reached the parking lot exit at almost the same time. I didn't leap off the last car and tackle him like in the movies. I might have, but he was still a step or two too far ahead of me.

I leaped down to the sidewalk and continued the chase. Then it took another block for me to run him down. When I did, I got one hand on his collar and another on his arm. I pushed him to the side. He slammed into the brick wall of the building at the corner, hitting it with both hands and his face. Hard. His grunt told me that.

I shoved my forearm between his shoulder blades and pinned him there while I kicked his feet and dug my handcuffs out of my jacket pocket. The little chain rattled as I wrenched his arms back, one at a time, and ratcheted the cuffs tightly around his wrists.

Once I had him cuffed, I started to go through his pockets. "You do drugs? There anything in here that'll stick me?"

"No," he managed to say, panting, his cheek pressed against the rough brick.

I found a gun in his right jacket pocket, a cheap, snub-nosed revolver. Then I retrieved the six bullets he'd also bought, thirty-eights, from his pants pocket.

By the time I was done, several people walking along Nationwide Boulevard noticed us. Most hurried on their way, pretending not to see, but others stopped to gawk.

"Come on," I said, yanking Mateo off the wall and waving my badge at the lookie-loos. "Got it … under control … Nothing to see … Go on."

Breathing heavily, I push-pulled Mateo back down the sidewalk and across the parking lot. I furtively eyeballed the cars I'd jumped on, relived not to see any damage.

"What's this all about?" he asked when his panting slowed enough so he could talk. "Who are you?"

"My name is Grace deHaviland. I'm the bounty hunter hired to bring your sorry ass in."

"Shit. Really?" His reaction was a cross between pissed off and open-mouthed awe.

"Really. You want to tell me about the gun?"

"No."

I yanked him to a stop. "Listen to me, you little shit. You're about ten minutes away from being locked inside a jail cell. Where you'll be for a very long time because of this stunt of yours. And don't think the D.A. isn't going to love adding a gun charge to you jumping bail—"

"Don't tell them about the gun. You can do that right?"

"No. And why would I?"

"Look. I'll go with you. I'll do whatever you want, but first, please, you've got to do something for me." His black eyebrows folded over his eyes, his swarthy, pleading face full of anguish. "I'm begging you. Please. Help me save my sister."

AN HOUR LATER, Mateo and I were in my car, a beautiful, restored, black 1978 Firebird, sitting outside a strip club called the Foxy Den. It was getting dark. The sun had receded from the sky, but the moon had yet to make an appearance. Mateo held a handkerchief to his cheek, where the scrapes were red and puffy. I bet they stung. Being shoved face-first into a brick wall will do that to you. The Chief's Special he'd bought from Dink was locked safely in my glove compartment, along with the six loose bullets.

I watched the neon outline of a dancing girl flash in three different positions on the black sign over the building we were watching. A dozen cars were parked near us. The windows were curtained so no one could see in, but the music was loud and heavy with a deep bass that thumped through the walls and reverberated up through the floorboards of my baby. Damn rap-crap.

"Okay, we're here," I said. "Now, tell me about your sister."

Mateo shifted in his seat. I'd removed the handcuffs. He sat with one leg pulled up Indian-style, facing me. His hands fidgeted in his lap. He talked fast. As if he had to beat the clock. "Rosario is my big sister. In high school, she started doing drugs. Her boyfriend, he hooked her on them." He shook his head. Angry and sad, his eyes gleamed with tears in the neon light.

I thought back to what Mrs. Lopez had said about Mateo. *He is good boy.* "This boyfriend? Was he the man you beat up outside the bar?"

"*Si*." He looked around as though he wanted to spit. "His name is Ramon Santiago. He is Rosario's pimp."

"Her pimp?" Now I wanted to spit. No wonder the boy beat the shit out of him. "She's in the trade?"

"*Si*. To pay for the drugs he gives her. That *puta* turned my sister into an addict, then he turned her into a whore."

I glanced at the club. A tricked-out SUV with 40-inch chrome wheels pulled into the lot. The bass-heavy hip-hop blaring from it stopped, and the halogen headlights switched off. Two be-boppers wearing oversized flannel shirts and baseball caps twisted askew headed for the club. When the door to the place opened, I spied a large bouncer sitting on a stool inside the doorway. Also, a good number of blacks and Latinos crowded around the bar and stage.

"What makes you think your sister is here?"

"It's where she works. Ramon told me before I…." Mateo couldn't put his deeds into words. "They make Rosario dance, and in between…she whores."

"Even with Ramon in the hospital?"

"*Si*, because he is not the *jefe,* the boss. Ramon. He recruits the girls. Gets them hooked on the drugs with his good looks and his promises until they are helpless, dependent. When they can't refuse him, he brings them here. To this place. To be whores for the drugs they now need."

Mateo had a surprisingly good understanding of how drug and prostitution rings operated. It also explained why Mateo wasn't satisfied with just beating the hell out of Ramon Santiago. He wanted something more. His end game was to rescue Rosario.

"That's why you bought the gun. To get your sister out?"

"I don't know where she lives. Her cell phone number does not work. The only way was to get the information from Ramon. I can't leave her to live this way. It will kill her." His dark eyes filled with sadness. The young man who was trying so hard to be tough suddenly looked so young, like a baby. "I wouldn't hurt anyone. The gun, it was for show." He licked his lips. "To make them listen."

Poor, naive kid, I thought. The people he was talking about would have laughed at him and his little gun. Then they would have blown him away. "You're an idiot, Mateo. You wouldn't have accomplished a thing except to get yourself killed, and maybe your sister too."

His face darkened with anger. "What do you know? You're just a stupid girl. I would have saved her," he insisted, "if you hadn't stopped me."

"No. You'd be dead. Now quiet. I've got a phone call to make."

Mateo twisted around and crossed his arms over his thin chest. He stared out the window, but I was sure he saw nothing except his own anger and frustration. "Go on. Call the cops. See if I care."

I ignored him, listening to the cell phone ring. Suzie Jensen picked up on the third ring, out of breath. "Did I catch you at a bad time?"

She panted. "If you had, I wouldn't have answered. Out for a run. Six miles."

"Good for you." I smiled. Suzie hated to exercise. "You feel like giving me a hand with something?"

There was a momentary pause. "What kind of trouble have you gotten into this time?"

I told her, and then I told her where she should meet us.

Thirty minutes later, Suzie tapped on the window of my Firebird. I had Mateo climb in the back so Suzie could slide into the passenger seat. "Mateo, this is Suzie Jensen. She's a deputy with the county Sheriff's Department."

He arched an eyebrow. "You must be kidding."

Suzie wore pink Uggs: black stockings: a denim mini-skirt, and a striped, long-sleeve shirt under a leather motorcycle vest with ragged sleeve holes. But I think it was the diamond-studded earrings rimming her ear, the nose stud, and her pieced eyebrow that caused Mateo to doubt her stated profession. Or it might have been her mousse-thick, spiky, butch blond hair.

Suzie took off the pink-lensed granny sunglasses she wore and smiled her infectious smile. "That better?"

"No. Whatever. You're still here to take me to jail."

"Eventually," I said. "But first, Suzie and I are going to see if your sister's inside. If she is, we'll figure out how we can help after that."

Mateo leaned forward like an eager dog, anxious. "What do you mean? You'll bring her out, won't you?"

"One step at a time. Let's see if she's even in there first. Then we'll see about getting her out." To Suzie, I said, "You ready?"

She nodded. "No, but when has that ever stopped us before?"

We got out. I leaned back through the open window and said to Mateo, "Sit tight. And remember, if you run, I'll just catch you again."

"I won't run. Grace?"

I turned.

He said, "Thank you."

I walked away with a lump in my throat. Damn kid.

Suzie and I headed across the parking lot. When I'd called her, she'd told me the department had a thick file on the Foxy Den. It was a haven for street gang drugs and prostitution, all of it run under the watchful eye of a gangbanger who called himself Dollar Biz.

"Tell me about this Dollar Biz," I asked now.

"He's a scary dude, Grace. He's thirty-five years old, arrested a few times when he was younger—drugs, assaults, guns—the usual for an up-and-coming gangbanger. He did some time, too, enough to earn his share of some street cred, but nothing recent. Since then, he's wised up. Now he keeps his distance from the business. Lets guys like Ramon Santiago do his dirty work. I doubt we'll get anything we can use to make a prostitution case against him."

"I'm not trying to make a case," I said, reaching for the door. That was one advantage of doing the work I do; making cases, civil rights, procedural law, none of that mattered to me. "My only interest is the girl, if she's here, and getting her out."

"Easier said than done." Suzie had a knack for understatement.

I pulled the door open and waved her in. "You first."

INSIDE, I WINCED at the incredibly loud and very bad dance music while I paid the cover charge to the bouncer. He stamped our hands. Like we'd want to come back in here again. Suzie slipped her arm around my waist and we sashayed over to the bar, creating quite a stir with the horn-toad degenerates and gangbangers leering across the bar, their tongues out and their fists full of dollars.

"Two drink minimum," the bartender shouted over what could only laughingly be called music.

"Beer," I shouted back.

He smacked four glass mugs of beer onto the wet bar and waited even after I handed him a twenty. "Seven-fifty each."

"Seriously?"

"Seriously."

I shook my head and dug out another twenty. I handed it to him, then plopped down on a barstool. I took a sip. The beer was warm and flat. The bastards should be arrested just for that.

Two girls danced on the carpeted stage behind the bar. Naked except for their glittering g-strings and spiked, do-me heels. They each wore a vacant expression as if the lights were on, but anything alive inside had shut down. Neither girl was Latina.

To Suzie, I said, "So?"

She took a casual glance around the bar, her gaze lingering for a moment on several people crowded around a booth in back. When she returned her attention to me, she flipped my hair back over my shoulder and leaned close as if to nuzzle my earlobe.

Instead, she whispered, "Back corner. Three baby gangstas holding court with a Snoop Dogg wannabe."

I took a sip of warm beer and then playfully pushed her away to take a look. "Got him."

"That's Dollar Biz."

All the men were African-American. And none of them except Biz looked old enough to drink. Two girls sat with Biz, one white, the other one black. Fake smiles were plastered on their made-up faces. Unable to sit still, they were buzzing on booze and cocaine or something worse.

I started to worry Rosario might not be around. "How long before we get vetted?"

"Already happening." Suzie took a sip of beer and grimaced. Her face was priceless. "Oh, that's awful."

The baby gangsta Biz sent over came at us with a swagger, wearing oversized cargo jeans and a heavy OSU football jacket. I could see the gun hitched to the elastic band of his boxers. He grinned, revealing a single gold-capped front tooth. The bling around his neck gleamed in the flashing disco lights.

"What's up, ladies," he said, waving a toothpick toward the dancers. "Them girls off the hook or what?"

Suzie gave him the up and down. "They're all right." She turned her back on him.

"All right?" He nearly choked. "You better check yourself, blondie. Them bitches are fine."

"Forget the eye candy," I said. "Who do we talk to about something more?" I looked past him and made eye contact with Biz, who sat checking us out. "Him?"

"No way, sista. I'm your man." He slapped his chest. "But we don't deal in dudes, you feel me?"

Suzie arched an eyebrow. "If we were in the market for guys, you think we'd come to a place like this?"

Jamal nearly swallowed his toothpick. "Okay, girl, Jamal reads you. We're nothing if not inclusive. Tell me your flavor. I'll see what we've got in inventory."

"Give me your choosin' fee," I said. Street lingo for what he'd charge for me to pick out a girl for sex. By asking first, I eliminated any chance of making a solicitation charge, eliminating the possibility we were cops. "If we like your stock....."

I let that hang. Inventory. Stock. These were human beings we were talking about.

He smiled wide. His gold tooth glimmered. He held up two fingers. Two hundred dollars.

"We want a Latina, like me."

"We?" He popped the toothpick back in his mouth and grinned, rolling it around with his thin, pink tongue. "Be extra for two. You flip me three Benjamins. We's got us a deal."

I pulled out three one-hundred-dollar bills and fanned them for him. "We've got a deal. If we approve of what you're offering."

"Oh, you'll approve. I guarantee it. Wait here, be right back." He swaggered back to Biz, leaned down, and whispered into his ear. They both glanced over at us, then started talking again. Biz nodded. He sucked in a lungful of smoke off his stogie, blowing a thick stream of blue smoke into the air.

"What do you think?" I asked.

Suzie took a sip of beer and groaned. "I think I need to stop agreeing to help you on these crazy cases of yours."

"Come on," I said. "You love it."

She harrumphed, then gave me a smile. She did love this shit.

Jamal finished talking with Biz and then trotted off to a door in the back. Biz focused all his attention on entertaining his party—talking and laughing and smoking his big cigar. A few minutes later, Jamal came back into the bar, tugging the stick-thin upper arms of two women. In the mind-numbing flash of multi-colored strobe lights, I couldn't tell if either one was Rosario. I'd only seen an old photograph of her once, and only for a few seconds. Even if one of them was the girl we were looking for, it meant we'd be leaving another poor girl behind with these *hijo de puta pendejos.*

"Here we go," I said, tapping Suzie's leg.

We slipped off our stools and met Jamal and the girls in the dining section among the S-shaped booths. With the flashing lights at our backs, I immediately saw one girl *was* Rosario. Though she was older and her face frightfully gaunt, I recognized the dark eyes and the once beautiful child I'd seen in the photographs at her mom's house.

I tried to ignore the empty look in her eyes. Like the dancers and the girls curled up in the booth beside Biz, whatever life had once lived inside these girls was gone. They were empty shells, nothing more. Meat, and we were treating them that way right now.

"She'll do," I said, pointing at Rosario, hating how callous I sounded.

Suzie nodded.

"Where?" I asked.

"We've got rooms in back. She'll show you." Jamal held out his hand. I put the three hundred dollars into it. "Thirty minutes," he said. "No more."

Jamal escorted the other girl away, back over to rejoin Biz, all smiles.

In a flat voice, Rosario said, "This way."

She led us to the back door, where Jamal had brought her from. She moved like an automaton: slow, measured, lifeless.

She opened the door to a brightly lit hallway. Hit by the stark light, I blinked. Two swinging doors to the left led into a kitchen area. I shuddered at the thought of eating anything cooked in a place like this. Along the right side of the passageway were two restroom doors, a utility closet, and at the end of the hall, a door marked "Stairs." Once the door swung closed behind us, Suzie went to work checking out the kitchen, then the bathrooms. The utility closet was locked. She came back into the hall. "Clear."

"Rosario. Wait." I reached for her arm, stopping her from heading to the back stairwell.

She turned. She had dark smudges under her eyes and finger-combed hair. She picked at it as if she had fleas. It took a concentrated effort for her to meet my gaze. Confused and suspicious, she slowly came to realize I shouldn't have known her name. "How…"

"We're not here to … you know." I waved over at the stairs. "We're here to talk. Mateo sent me. He's worried about you."

"Mateo," she said slowly. "Matty?"

Suzie watched us while keeping one eye on the door to the bar. If Biz or one of his baby gangsters decided to come back to take a leak, or something else, we'd be in trouble.

"Yes. Matty," I said. "He asked us to come get you. He's waiting outside."

"Matty's here?"

Impatient, Suzie said, "Yes. He's here. We have to go."

I shared her anxiety. The last thing I wanted was to tangle with four idiot gangbangers with guns. So, of course, Rosario chose that moment to go nuts on us.

She pulled away, shouting. "No. No! Matty. He can't be here. He can't see me like this. Get away from me!"

She shoved me away and ran for the exit, heading back to the bar. I leaped to get in front of her, to hold the door shut before she got through it. But I was too late. "Shit."

Rosario ran through the door, screaming.

Suzie said, "Here we go."

"You think there's a back way out of here?"

"Probably, but we'll be dead before we find it."

"You're saying you want to face them head-on?"

"You got a better idea?"

I didn't. I dropped to one knee, tore my back-up 9-mil Sig Sauer from my ankle holster, and stood up again. Keeping the nine in my right hand, my weak hand, I pulled out my .45 and held it in my left. Feeling too much like Rambo, I said, "You going to call it in?"

"And say what?" Suzie asked. She had her Lady Smith—a small .38 revolver—out and ready. She was right. We couldn't prove a solicitation charge. And, as far as we knew, no other laws had been broken. That was about to change as we faced four, I was sure, very heavily armed men in the next room.

Suzie took hold of the pull handle. "Ready?"

I nodded, holding both weapons in the air. "Ready."

She yanked the door open.

I charged through.

The light from the service hallway knifed through the dark bar. I moved quickly to the right to give Suzie room to come out to my left. *Here we go again.*

Jamal held Rosario by her arms, shaking her, yelling. Biz's other two gangbangers stood with him. They pointed at us, drawing guns from under their oversized clothes. Biz remained seated. Having pushed his girls aside, he leaned forward as if he were center ice at a Blue Jackets' game and a fight had just broken out. Something unexpected. And entertaining.

Jamal tossed Rosario aside and drew his Glock. "What the fuck's going on?"

We had three guns pointed at us. Then the bouncer came off his seat at the front door, drawing a weapon from under his jacket. Make that four guns.

I lined my nine up on the bouncer's forehead and aimed the .45 at Jamal's chest. Suzie covered the other two men. Four against two, almost a fair fight.

Rosario sat crumbled on the floor, tears wet on her cheeks, wailing and trembling, too scared to move, too strung out to do anything but cry.

Biz sat back in the plush black leather booth and smiled. His white teeth gleamed. The swirling, colored lights splashed over his oily black skin. He appeared amused. "Anybody wanna explain to me what the fuck's going on?"

"We're not looking for trouble," I said.

"Funny, as how you've got it, *senorita*." Biz slapped his hands down on his knees. With a put-upon, exaggerated groan came to his feet, giving us a *tsk-tsk* shake of his head.

"Don't do anything stupid," Suzie said.

"I would say it's you two who's doing stupid. Wouldn't you agree?"

I took that to be a rhetorical question.

In her non-shooting hand, Suzie held out her badge, waving it at Biz. "I'm a sheriff's deputy. All we're interested in is the girl."

Biz didn't move except for his eyes. They settled on Rosario, sitting on folded legs, crying. "What's she to you?"

"She's been reported missing," I lied. "We're here to make sure she's okay. And to bring her home."

The dancers had stopped dancing and were cowering in the space between the stage and the bar. The gangbangers and degenerates scrambled off their stools and were crouched behind the bar, hidden away from the gunfire sure to start any minute. They watched like mole rats, their beady little eyes at bar level, their little fingers clutching the bar's black padding.

"What if she don't wanna go?" Biz asked with a sneer.

"Careful what you say next," Suzie warned. "Right now, we have no reason to arrest you—"

"Because all those guns you're pointing at us are registered and legally owed," I said. We weren't interested in gun charges or prostitution arrests or anything like that. Right now, we just wanted to get out of there alive.

Suzie nodded. "And Rosario Lopez, she is not connected to you in any way that we know or can prove." Suzie drilled Biz with her eyes. "Unless you lay some type of claim to her now."

"Or try to stop us from taking her out of here," I said.

"If you don't do that," Suzie said. "We have no reason to do anything except leave."

"With the girl," I added.

Biz smiled. Slowly and maliciously. Then he started clapping. "Nicely played, ladies. But what if the girl don't wanna go with you? What then?" To Rosario, he said, "What do you say, Rose? You wanna go with these crazy bitches, or you wanna stay here? Where it's safe. With Biz and the boys?"

Rosario lifted her head. She looked at Biz, then at Suzie and me. She had to make a decision, and we all waited. "I...I...."

Then everything went all to hell.

The front door swung open, and Mateo charged in, waving the cheap Chief's Special around. The little son of a bitch must have broken into my glove compartment.

If this stunt didn't kill him, I would. I shouted, "Mateo! No!"

Suzie called out over the rap-crap still playing. "Everybody stay cool."

I held my breath, waiting, knowing this was going to end badly. Very, very badly.

"Who's 'dis?" Biz demanded.

"Rosario's brother. He's why we're here."

Biz looked at Mateo, then looked down at Rosario. A minute passed. My hands were sweaty. My arms started to ache. When he stepped over to Rosario, I tracked him with my .45. "Don't do anything stupid," I warned.

He gave me an *I-want-to-kill-you* look, then took a fistful of Rosario's hair and yanked her to her feet. She screamed and clawed at his hand, scrambling to get her legs under her.

"Let her go, Biz."

"It's up to her." To Rosario, he said, "What's it gonna be, girl? You hanging with Biz, or you going with them?"

Everything focused on her. Time stood still.

"Make up your mind, girl," Biz said.

"Rosie. Please," Mateo begged.

Her eyes filled with tears. "Matty, please. Go."

He shook his head. "What? No!"

Biz looked at Suzie and me. "Youse got your answer. Now, get that little punk-ass the hell out my club. Youse got five seconds."

Suzie tried one more time. "Rosario. Think about what you're doing. We can help you. Come with us."

Rosario shook her head, tears falling down her cheeks, her face so full of anguish it made my heart hurt. "I...can't."

Mateo rushed forward. "No!"

"Stop him!" Biz bellowed. "Now!"

"No!" Suzie stepped between Jamal and his boys and me and Mateo, her gun aimed at Biz.

I intercepted Mateo's charge, grabbing him around the waist. "Come on. There's nothing more we can do." He struggled against me, small and wiry and surprisingly strong. "Come on, Mateo. We tried. We have to go."

"No," he cried, but reality dampened his fire—doused by his sister's inability to help herself, seeing her that way.

"Get him out of here." Biz yelled, "And yo, bitch."

I'd been moving Mateo slowly toward the front door. I stopped, and half turned.

"That's right, you," Biz said. "I know who you are. You ain't no Sheriff's cop. You're that bounty hunter bitch. Runs around town jamming brothers up. You think you can come in here, all up in my crib, without no retribution? Ain't happening. You feeling me?"

"Grace, don't," Suzie said, her tone stern. She nodded her head toward the exit. "Go."

"That's right, go," Biz yelled. "But this shit ain't over. Not by a long shot. You hear me?"

Suzie raised her gun, aiming it firmly at Biz's chest. If we were going down, she made it clear he would be the first to go with us. "Yes, it is, Biz."

He smiled. "For now, sweet pea. For now."

We made it outside without any more trouble. I had one arm around Mateo's waist. Suzie closed in on his other side. He walked with his face in his hand, sobbing. At the car, he leaned against the fender.

"Mateo," I said, searching for the right words. What could I say? "I'm sorry."

"Why? Why wouldn't she come with us? I don't understand."

"She's not ready," Suzie said. "His hold over her is too strong." Suzie'd had experience dealing with substance abusers. Her mother had been a raging alcoholic who'd died from the disease. Suzie knew its grip and its pain all too well. "She's got to reach rock bottom before she can start to help herself."

Mateo's head snapped up. He pointed furiously at the Foxy Den. "Whoring herself for that *puta*, that's not rock bottom?"

Suzie sighed. "Not for her. Not yet."

Mateo shook his head, not comprehending.

I took the gun still in his hand and handed it to Suzie. "We should get out of here."

She looked back at the Foxy Den. "Don't take Biz lightly, Grace. He's a dangerous man who makes good on his threats."

"I won't," I said, but he'd have to get in line. The list of people who've taken me off their Christmas lists was a long one. "Come on."

"Where?" Mateo asked.

"Well," I said, hating to bring it up. "You still have a date with a judge."

He looked at me with empty eyes. "Fine. Whatever."

"Hey." I took him by the shoulders and shook him. "You listen to me."

He blinked, the last of his tears slipping off his long eyelashes.

"Your sister made her choice. Tonight. And long ago. Maybe someday she'll fix that, maybe she won't. Either way, there's nothing you can do about it. That's all on her."

"Okay. Yeah. So."

"So. You have a choice too," I told him. "Don't let your mother lose both of you, Mateo. That you can do something about."

"Yeah." Defiant but without any spirit. "How?"

"By doing the right thing," Suzie said. She gave him an encouraging smile.

"Mateo, you beat a man into a coma, and you jumped bail. You need to answer for that." I handed him a business card. "This is a defense lawyer I know, one of the best around. She can argue that you acted in defense of your sister. Plead extenuating circumstances when you went after Santiago. She'll get it pled down to a misdemeanor. You'll probably get probation for a first offense. The D.A. will go along with that. My friend, she's very persuasive."

"Especially," Suzie added, holding up the illegally purchased Chief's Special, "in exchange for your testimony against Dink. That's a case the D.A.'ll love to prosecute."

I opened the car door and folded the seat forward so Mateo could climb into the back. When he was in, Suzie circled around the passenger side. Over the roof, she gave me a quizzical look. It said *you think the kid will be all right?*

I shrugged. Only time would tell. I gave the Foxy Den a final look. My heart hurt thinking about the destructive power drugs can have on a person. The hold they have. There Rosario was, and all those other girls, deep in the bowels of hell by anybody's standard, and she was too hooked, too afraid, to grab hold of the lifeline we offered her. Maybe she didn't recognize it for what it was. Maybe she was just too far gone to care.

I climbed into the car and started it up. Suzie pointed at the hole in the glove compartment where the lock cylinder had been. From the backseat, Mateo called out, "Don't worry, I'll fix it."

"Damn right you will," I said, driving away and wondering if Mateo was talking about my glove compartment or his life. I smiled, hoping he meant both.

###

KICKIN' IT SOUTH OF THE BORDER

Matamoros, Mexico

"*HA VISTO USTED* a este hombre*?*" I asked the desk clerk at our hotel, showing him a black-and-white mug shot of Harold Weismann. Its resemblance to Mel Gibson's infamous mug shot from a few years back was uncanny. Weismann was a bit fleshier, perhaps, but like Gibson, he'd been arrested for drunk driving—in Toledo, Ohio, not California—and after getting belligerent with the arresting officer, he made the ultimate stupid mistake: He took a swing at the cop.

That bought Weismann twenty-four hours in the Lake County lockup, and it's funny how the cops can keep losing a guy's paperwork. When he finally got before a judge, he pled not guilty, posted bail, and was released. Unemployed, Weismann had apparently fallen on hard times. A casualty of the auto industry's implosion a few years back, he'd been laid off when the automobile supply company he worked for went belly up. Unable to find another job, he took up drinking—with an anger and depression chaser.

"Grace, what are you doing?"

I had my back to Suzie Jensen, my best friend, and traveling companion. Suzie didn't happen to speak Spanish, so I hoped she'd think I was asking for directions to the town's hottest nightclub.

"Is that a mug shot?" she asked, knowing me well enough to know it was.

I felt like a kid caught with my hand in the cookie jar.

"*Un momento, por favor.*"

I steered Suzie well away from the counter. Mariachi music drifted in from the bar filling the sandstone and tile lobby. To Suzie, I said, "Now, don't go all postal on me, okay?"

Best friends since high school, Suzie and I joined the Sheriff's Department together when we were all of twenty-one—twelve years ago. I lasted less than two years, but Suzie stuck it out and had been with the department ever since. Meanwhile, I'd turned to bounty hunting to make a living.

Her vibrant blue eyes glared cold daggers at me. "You can't do this, Grace. It's against the law."

She was right. It's illegal to extricate a bail jumper from a foreign country. If I did that, that would be my bad ... but there was nothing wrong with me using a little friendly persuasion to get the guy back over the border. Right?

Suzie ran her hand through her short, spiky blonde hair. The diamond stud she wore in her nose caught the light and gleamed. She paced. "Damn it, Grace. I should have known."

"Suzie." I grabbed her shoulders to stop her pacing. "He's an out-of-work human resources manager. He rented a car using his own credit card. Used it to reserve a room here. He's an idiot." I was talking fast, knowing I had only seconds to win her over. "A day or two tops. Once I've got him, we take him over the border to Brownsville. I turn him in there, and for the rest of the week, it's beaches and sunshine and Pina Coladas. I promise."

"Two days. You promise?"

"Scout's honor." I held up my hand.

We returned to the desk clerk. I held up the mug shot again. "This man. He's staying here. Yes?"

The clerk took the photograph, lifted his glasses, looked at it squinting, then shrugged.

He didn't say no, so I asked, "What room?"

He gave me a pained expression and shook his head. "*Lo siento.*" I am sorry. Excuse me. "I cannot tell you this, *senorita.* Hotel rules."

Suzie hissed, "Shit."

She held out her badge. "This is official police business. What room?"

The badge failed to impress. "*Policia. Catels drogas.*" Police. Drug cartels. He shrugged. "I am not afraid of them. Or of you. Tomorrow. Manager is here. Speak to him." The clerk busied himself with something behind the counter, concentrating on it with great focus. Noticing we were still there, he added, "Good day."

It was my turn to curse.

"Now what?" Suzie asked.

The mariachi music drew me toward the bar. I needed a drink. My answer wouldn't please her. "He's staying here, so we wait."

"I knew you were going to say that." She made a face. It was not a happy one.

"We can wait in the bar."

"Fine. But you're buying."

I checked my watch. Five-thirty p.m. What does a fifty-two-year-old unemployed HR manager do while on the lam in Mexico? And why Matamoros—a place not exactly topping the chart of desirable vacation spots these days? Few border towns were these days, in light of the devastating cartel violence going on down here.

I ordered two Coronas and settled at the table Suzie found for us. From where we sat, I could see the front desk and main entrance through the potted plants and wicker chairs and coffee tables arranged under a low-hung, slow-turning ceiling fan. As far as surveillance went, we could've—and certainly have—done worse.

"Excuse me, *senoritas*." A kid I guessed to be about thirteen or fourteen with dark curly hair, swarthy skin, and a bright smile full of mischievous confidence approached our table. "I overhear your inquiries at the front desk. You *policia*?"

"Yes," Suzie said. The kid eyed the line of earrings rimming her outer ear and her black nail polish with some doubt. She insisted. "We are," she insisted. "What do you want?"

Still mad at me, she was taking it out on the kid. I gave her a *backdown, girl* look. Me playing good cop. Now there was a switch. "What can we do for you?" I asked.

He cleared his throat and held out his hand. "*Fotographia d'el hombre*. I see it?"

Suzie and I exchanged a glance. I fished the mug shot out of my jacket pocket and showed it to him.

"This man, yes, he here with *su esposa*—he wife." The kid smiled. "I take you to them. Fifty dollar."

Suzie almost spurted out her beer. "Fifty bucks!"

The kid took it in stride. "This man. He is important, no?"

"Yes," I admitted, taking a twenty from a fold of cash I carried in my jeans. I handed it to him. "The rest when I'm sure the room is his."

I expected the kid to scamper away with my money, settling for the twenty as the best he could con out of us. He surprised me: He said, "Follow me."

Suzie shook her head. She was still angry at me, but her interest had been piqued. She finished her beer and stood up. Unwilling to leave a drink half finished, I did the same, tossing a couple of dollars on the table.

The kid led us up a back stairwell, out of sight of the front desk, to the third floor. The hallway was clear. The walls were scuffed and in need of a fresh coat of paint while the air smelled of tequila, suntan lotion, and faintly of vomit—lingering reminders of spring breaks past, of better times for the hotel and for Matamoros. A bit nervous about what we were getting into, I patted the small Beretta in the pancake holster I wore on my hip.

The kid slowed, then came to a stop at a door midway down the hall. His air of confidence evaporated. Over his shoulder, he said, "This not good."

He was right. I touched his arm and gently pulled him back from the door. The doorframe around the card key locking mechanism was freshly splintered. I whispered, "This is the room?"

He nodded. His eyes wide.

"Wait here." Suzie darted to the far side of the damaged door. When she was in place, I pulled the Beretta. She stared at my little .25. "What are you doing with *that*?" She hissed.

"What? You mean you *didn't* bring a gun?" I couldn't imagine.

"No, I didn't bring a gun. I brought a bikini. You said vacation, remember? On vacation, I bring bikinis, not firearms." It was amazing how much anger she could project with the quietest of whispers.

I smiled. "I'll go in first, then."

Easing open the door, I peered into the room. A mirrored closet lined the facing wall. In the mirror, I could see most of the small space. There was a single king-sized bed and two-night stands. The sliders out to a balcony were ajar, letting the sound of outside traffic in.

I stepped into the short hallway leading to the room. At the corner, I poked my head around and located the open door to the bathroom. Suzie followed me in. While I covered her, she carefully spread wide the closet doors. A few shirts and trousers hung on the rod—a single yellow dress. A black suitcase lay on the floor, but nothing else.

I signaled my intent to search the bathroom. Suzie nodded and moved toward the sliders, checking to see if someone lay in wait, hiding on the floor beside the bed or outside on the balcony. The bathroom was small—and empty.

I holstered my weapon. "Clear."

Suzie cried out, "Oh, Christ!"

I re-drew my weapon and rushed to her side.

She had crouched on one knee beside the bed and shouted, not to me but to the kid gawking in from the doorway. "Get an ambulance! Now!"

A middle-aged woman lay on the floor. Suzie had tilted the woman's head to one side and pressed her hands to the unresponsive woman's neck. Her throat and Suzie's hands were coated in blood, while more blood pooled under the vic's head, soaking the old, brown carpet and matted the woman's short graying hair. Her throat had been slashed, but…

"She's alive! Get me some towels!"

I grabbed a fistful of towels from the bathroom. Suzie pressed them to the gaping wound. The woman tried to speak, desperate in her attempt.

"It's okay," Suzie said. "We're the police. From the U.S."

I held the woman's shoulder and leaned in closer. "What? What is it?"

"My son," she gasped, gurgling blood. "Help… my son."

THIRTY MINUTES LATER, the paramedics had come and gone with their patient. Left behind were torn gauze-pad wrappers, snipped first-aid tape, a drying bloodstain, and a cop named Delgado. He wore dark green fatigues and a Marine-style watch cap and carried an M4 carbine. In his hands, he held a pad and pen, ready to take notes as he questioned us in halting English. "You say you do not know this woman?" We'd established the victim was Dorothy Weismann from her driver's license, found in her purse in the nightstand drawers.

"No." Suzie sat on the end of the bed wiping at her hands with a towel even though she'd scrubbed them pink, and all trace of blood had been removed. Still, she kept examining her hands and wiping.

I explained to Captain Delgado why we were there and how we came to discover the woman, keeping the kid, who was gone with the rest of my fifty, out of it. Captain Delgado of the *Policía Federal Preventiva* pushed his cap back and stared at his notebook with a knotted expression. As if what he read there puzzled him. "This Harold Weismann, he's a fugitive from your U.S. justice?"

"Yes, he is."

"And you come here to Matamoros to bring him back? To violate international law?"

Did he really expect me to admit my intention to break the law? "To talk to him. To convince him to come back home on his own. No force." Yeah, right.

Still wiping her hands, Suzie said, "I'm here on vacation."

"Do you think he did this thing?" He pointed his pen at the wide blood stain. "To his wife?"

"I don't know. Is she conscious? Will she live?"

It was Delgado's turn to say, "I do not know." He followed that with: "You are guests of the hotel?"

Suzie stood up. "Yes."

"Good." Delgado tucked his notebook in his back pocket. "Stay and enjoy the pool. The nightlife Matamoros has to offer. Until we sort this business out." His smile grew somber. "So we are clear—that is not a request."

"We understand," I said. He was ordering us not to leave town.

Suzie responded with a shot at me. "And so *we're* clear. This is the worse vacation I've *ever* had."

THREE CORONAS AND two hours later, Suzie returned to the hotel bar where I had the place to myself except for the bartender and a twelve-year-old busboy wiping down tables. *Abrázame Y Bésame* played on the jukebox. Certainly not the happening nightspot Delgado might have suggested had we asked. Of course, the recently escalating, horrific violence between the drug cartels and the Mexican government made Matamoros, and many of the border towns in Mexico, less the travel destination than it had been in years past. The nearly deserted streets were a testament to that.

What was the draw for the Weismanns? The question nagged at me.

Suzie sat and took the Corona I nursed. She finished it.

"Still mad?" I asked.

"Yes." She waved the empty bottle in the air signaling the bartender for two more. She'd changed into a red tank top, a plaid work shirt tied at the waist, blue jeans, and black Keds. She'd exchanged the diamond stud in her nose for a silver hoop. I was in the same black jeans and sleeveless tee shirt under my leather jacket I'd worn that morning driving into Mexico from Corpus Christi.

The busboy delivered our two beers. "A few more of these, and maybe I'll forgive you." Suzie took a long pull on her Corona, then sat forward, lowering her voice. "I called Tolman."

James Lee Tolman was the chief deputy of patrol for the Sheriff's Department back home. He was also Suzie's boss—and had been mine too. Before he fired me.

"What'd he have to say?"

"You mean after, 'What kind of god-damned trouble has Grace gotten you into this time?'"

I drank my beer. "Yes. After that."

"He said the Weismanns do have a kid." She read from a page she'd torn off a pad of hotel notepaper. "A twenty-two-year-old son—his name's Aaron. He's been arrested twice. A shoplifting beef when he was sixteen and a minor drug possession charge. Weed. Two years ago. While he was going to OSU."

"A college kid smoking dope. Imagine that." I had to smile.

"Tolman had the detectives do a little checking. Turns out the kid dropped out of college last year. The registrar's office said it was for financial reasons."

"Daddy's not bringing home the bacon anymore."

Suzie took a sip of beer. "That's my guess. Could piss a kid off."

"Well, I did some digging too." I'd reached the bottom of my Corona and considered another one but decided against it. "I spoke to Book." Eugene Booker was an investigator with the Ohio Bureau of Criminal Identification & Investigation, commonly called BCI. He and I had an on-again, off-again thing going—lately, more on than off, I was happy to say. "He dug through some less-than-public records for me and found out Weismann took a second mortgage on his house."

"To pay his bail?"

"Interestingly, no. The house was signed over as collateral." The bail bondsman who'd hired me had run a lien search on the mortgage, and it came up clean. If she knew Weismann had taken out new paper on it, she'd flip.

"How much did he get in the second mortgage?" Suzie asked.

"Two-hundred-thirty-five-thousand dollars."

Suzie whistled. "Two-hundred K. I could start a nice life down here with that kind of capital."

"Except that is not what he's using it for." Captain Delgado said, entering the bar from the hotel lobby. He pulled out a chair, sat down at our table, and snapped his fingers. The busboy brought him a mixed drink, something the bartender obviously had ready for the cop. Delgado took a sip and smacked his lips. "Ah."

When he was done savoring his drink, I asked him, "What's he using the money for?"

"To pay off the Munoz Mateos drug cartel."

Skepticism laced my response. "You're saying a fifty-two-year-old, out-of-work, mid-level manger like Harold Weismann is tied up with a Mexican drug cartel?"

Delgado sat back, took another sip, and smiled smugly. "No, my pretty American *senorita*. Nor did Weismann come down to Mexico to escape your American justice." He looked over at Suzie. "Or to start a new life.

"He came to Mexico to pay ransom money to the Mateos cartel. Two-hundred-thousand American dollars in exchange for his worthless, drug-dealing son's life."

"OKAY. HOW DID you come up with that?" I asked.

We drove west into the desert, passengers in Captain Delgado's radio car. He aimed the cruiser at top speed down a paved ribbon of inky, unlit blacktop, with little around us but dirt, rocks, and cacti. Suzie and I sat together in the back, both of us wondering what the hell I'd gotten us involved in this time.

"Mrs. Weismann regained consciousness at the hospital." Delgado twisted around in the front seat. "She and her husband came here to rescue their son from the Mateos cartel."

"Why does he need rescuing?" Suzie asked.

"The boy's running drugs for them," I guessed. "And something went wrong."

"*Si*. According to his *madre*, he is good boy," Delgado answered. "But he got involved in drugs to raise cash for the family. In their time of need." His father's unemployment situation. "She said he hoped to make enough so he could return to school. American education is very expensive, I understand."

"So, what happened?"

"She told me her son got ripped off. Selling to students on campus—his merchandise was stolen. He came down here to explain. The Mateos contacted the mother and the father and told them to bring the money Aaron owed them or be prepared to receive the boy's body. In pieces."

"Two hundred thousand?" I guessed.

"That is correct."

"Then they'll let the boy go?" Suzie asked, hopefully.

"So they say." He didn't sound convinced.

"Is that usually how these things go down here?"

He glanced in the rearview mirror. Our eyes locked. "No, *senorita*, it is not."

I glanced over at Suzie, more sorry than ever I'd dragged her into this. She shrugged.

The thing I've learned about Suzie after all these years is—she's an adrenaline junkie. The more exciting, the more dangerous, the more over-the-edge things get, the better she liked it. Of course, first comes the bitching about my getting her involved in one of my kooky cases, but then, when things heat up like they had now, she gets all into it, gung-ho and having the time of her life—all the while watching my back, while I watch hers. It's the nature of our friendship.

"Did Mrs. Weismann know where her husband might be now?"

"He left her to go to the drop location given to them by the kidnappers. That is where we are going now."

"They knew the Weismanns had the money and were willing to pay the ransom?" That bothered me.

"Apparently so," Delgado said.

"Then why slice open the woman's throat?"

"To leave no loose ends, perhaps. Or as a warning to others who might try ripping them off." He shrugged. "Maybe because they enjoy it. It is that way with them sometimes, sad to say."

We drove on in silence. The drop was to take place at an old ranch house about an hour's drive from Matamoros. We passed rolling desert folds filled with tumbleweeds and cactus and not much else. A dark mountain backdrop stood out dimly against a clear night sky. You don't see sky like that back home. Another couple of miles and Delgado turned off onto a rutted dirt road, the property sectioned off by miles of raw, split rail fence.

"You seem to know where you're going," Suzie commented, looking out the window.

Dust clouds billowed up around the car. Just beyond the car's headlights, the road forked to the left. The expansive mountain range blotted out the stars and cast dim shadows over a black landscape. The terrain felt vast and empty. And depressingly lonely.

"We know this site. It has been used by the Mateos cartel before."

The prospect of running into people capable of doing what had been done to Dorothy Weismann didn't sit well with me. "You have others coming out to meet us? Other police?"

Delgado didn't answer at first. When he did, he shifted. As if uncomfortable. "No, *senorita*, I do not."

The hairs on the back of my neck stood on end. Suzie shot me a look. "What are you planning to do out here then, exactly?" Concern raising the hairs on the back of my neck.

He glanced back at me in the mirror, then concentrated on the road ahead. "I do not believe the Mateos will still be here. We have nothing to be concerned about. The exchange, if it took place, took place this afternoon, many hours earlier. We are here to search for clues. And to recover Harold Weismann's body if he is not still alive."

"But what if they *are* still here?" Suzie demanded. "What then?"

"We surveil, gather intelligence. Then, as you Americans say, we call for backup." He cleared his throat. What he said next, he said with difficulty. "You must understand. *Policia* in my country are not, how shall I say … as trustworthy as those in your country. The work is dangerous. Many who are dedicated, who want to do the right thing, end up dead. The pay is another difficulty. The amount one can earn working with the drug cartels is much more … appealing than what one earns…."

He let it go, his point made. "Calling in would alert the Mateos we were on to them, on our way. This I did not want."

Delgado flicked off the car's lights and slowed. I leaned forward, wishing I could wipe off the dust-filmed windows. To our left, a low, dark ranch house sat at the grassy base of the mountains. Beyond the house was a barn with an open hayloft on the second level, a latticework timber windmill, and several split rail pens for housing farm animals. What kind? I had no clue since the pens were now empty.

"How *Wizard of Oz,*" Suzie said dryly.

"Sure, but this isn't Kansas," I answered her. "Looks deserted."

"As I assumed it would be," Delgado pointed out. He pulled to the side of the road before yet another rutted dirt path, this one leading toward the house. "We'll go in on foot from here."

He opened the door and got out, taking the M4 carbine with him. I noticed the dome light didn't go on. Delgado knew what he was doing.

"Wait a minute."

"Yes?"

"We're not armed," I said. A lie. Having my undeclared Beretta with me was illegal. I wasn't about to let anyone know I had it without good reason. "What if we encounter a problem? Don't you have something we could use?"

Delgado shook his head, not even considering it. "I cannot issue firearms to foreign tourists. It would be…frowned upon."

"So would getting us shot," Suzie said, too low for Delgado to hear clearly.

"Excuse me, *senorita*?"

"I said, let's do this. I've got a vacation to get started."

We walked, in single file, down the quarter-mile dirt road to the end of the spilt rail fencing. A car sat parked in front of the plank-board, rustic ranch house, a late model Chevy that had seen better days. Weismann's maybe?

The place looked deserted. "Now what?"

"We check the house first," Delgado said.

Crouching, he headed for the window to the right of the front door while I trotted a few steps behind. Suzie veered off toward the barn, unnoticed by Delgado, who sidled up to one side of a living room window. I took the other. The window had no coverings: no curtains, no blinds. The interior was dark and entirely still. Before we moved on to the next window, Suzie whistled to catch our attention.

At the barn door, she waved. We hurried over quietly and joined her. "I heard breathing inside. Low. Raspy," she said.

I took up a position opposite Suzie, and we grabbed the barn door handles. To Delgado, I whispered, "We open. You go in."

He nodded. He held the carbine tightly.

Suzie and I split the large, heavy doors, which slid open smoothly on iron tracks. Delgado charged in, following the bluish swath of moonlight we let inside. Suzie and I slipped in behind him, keeping to the shadows. The floor was dirt and carpeted with hay. The musty smell of barn animals lay heavy in the air.

A hardback chair sat in the middle of the barn with a man bound to it. His arms and torso were duct-taped to the chair's straight back. His legs taped to the front legs. His head hung so his chin rested on his chest. Blood soaked his clothes, and his labored breathing told me he'd suffered a severe beating and perhaps internal injuries. Without needing to examine his face, I knew we'd found my jumper, Harold Weismann.

Delgado moved to check each of the barn stalls while Suzie and I crowded around the injured man. "Mr. Weismann," I said, trying to roust him. "My name is Grace deHaviland. This is Suzie Jensen. We're from Ohio. We're here to help you."

Suzie put a hand on his thigh. He flinched.

"Easy."

He brought his head up. His eyes were swollen shut, lacerations marred his face, which was black and blue and swollen; blood crusted his nose and his mouth, hardening in the bristles of his day-old stubble. He grunted as he tried to open one eye. The beating he'd endured had been vicious. And prolonged.

Suzie asked, "Who did this to you?"

He moved his head in Suzie's direction. His dry tongue protruded from between bloody, split lips. I saw he had lost at least one tooth. The rest were coated in blood. "Mateos thugs. Trying to get...back my son."

"Didn't you bring them the money?"

He croaked out a hoarse laugh, then coughed. "Told them...told 'em...they get money when I...get my son."

"They did not like hearing that," Delgado said to our backs.

I turned, instantly realizing we'd fucked up. I knew what we'd face.

Delgado had the M4 carbine leveled directly at Suzie and me.

"You're in on it."

With a humorless smile, Delgado said, "*Si.*"

Suzie and I straightened up. We each took a step away from Weismann, widening the gap between us all. I raised my hands, keeping them out in the open, demonstrating I wasn't armed. I nodded toward Weismann but spoke to Delgado. "You did this."

Delgado ground his teeth in anger. "He was supposed to come bringing the money."

"I knew you'd... double-cross me. Told him. I...I'd tell him where the money was..."

"When he brought your son here," Suzie guessed.

"That's right," Weismann breathed. "I'm still waiting."

Weismann had proved to be tougher than he looked. I took another step to the right. If Delgado started shooting now, he'd have to choose among three targets. "What's the deal, Captain? Where's Aaron?"

"Is he still alive?" Suzie asked.

"He's alive." Delgado cocked his head, hearing something. I heard it, too. A car rolling slowly to a stop outside. The sound was followed by a door opening, then another. "That's him now."

I caught Suzie's eye.

She nodded. *Ready.*

I returned a tight smile. *Good girl.*

"So, why bring us out here?" I asked, directing Delgado's attention back to me.

"Mind if I put my hands down?"

Cocky, he nodded. "You *Americanos* have a saying. Keep your friends close—"

I finished the old saying. "And your enemies closer."

"We could not allow you to cause trouble. Not until we concluded our…." He glanced at Weismann with contempt. "…business. If he or his woman had told me where he'd hidden the money…." Delgado spit into the dirt. "But she was a stubborn as he is."

"Juan?" A thickly-accented voice called from outside.

Delgado made the mistake of twisting around toward the half-open barn door. Suzie lunged. He swung the M4 carbine in her direction. But I was even faster.

I got to him before he could squeeze off a shot and dug the business end of my Beretta into the hollow behind his ear. His surprise was apparent.

I whispered, "I'll blow your head off."

His expression told me he believed me, which was good. I pulled his hand from the carbine's trigger. He let the weapon go. Suzie grabbed the gun and turned it on him.

"*Puta!*"

"You have no idea," Suzie said.

Quickly, I pulled Delgado to the right side of the barn doors. Suzie trotted over to the left. I shoved Delgado against the rough-hewn wall. "One more sound," I whispered as menacingly as I knew how, "and you're a dead man."

I aimed the Beretta at the open door, high. Suzie held the carbine low, tight against her hip. With only the long rectangle of moonlight splashing across the barn floor for light, we were almost impossible to see. Even better, Delgado's compatriots were so overconfident they walked straight in, holding between them a young man I took to be Aaron.

With the element of surprise on our side, and gun barrels pressed into their temples, they offered no resistance. We stripped them of their weapons and dropped them to their knees. We had them interlock their hands behind their heads. Suzie stood guard over them while I helped Aaron cut his father loose.

"You okay?" I asked as we ripped the last of the duct tape from the beaten man's legs and helped him to his feet. He wobbled. Aaron looped his father's arm around his shoulder and held him up, supporting him. Weismann smiled weakly at his son. "I am now.

"My wife?" He glared over at Delgado. "He said...."

"She's okay," I told him. "She's in the hospital. She's hurt, but she's going to be fine."

"Thank God." He squeezed his son again, then said, "Who are you? How can I ever thank you?"

I felt like a heel, but I had to tell him. "My name is Grace deHaviland. I'm a bounty hunter hired to bring you back to the States. Back to Ohio."

"Oh." His smile faltered. "You understand why I did what I did? I wasn't actually running."

"Yes. I understand. You understand that doesn't change what I have to do."

He pulled his son into a deep embrace. Tears glistened in his bloodshot eyes. "You saved my son's life, Ms. deHaviland. I'll be happy to do whatever you want."

I nodded, watching the two of them. I thought how wonderful it must feel to have a supportive family. It was something I knew nothing about. I glanced over at Suzie and smiled. But I did know about having the support of a good friend. I went over to her. "What about you? You happy now?"

She gave me a look. The one that said: *How can I stay mad at you*? I get that one a lot.

Suzie held up a finger. "Beach." Held up a second finger. "Sunshine." And a third. "Pina Coladas. After that, we'll see."

I smiled. "The least I can do."

###

FATAL TRYST

Tryst n: *an agreement (as between lovers) to meet: to make or keep a tryst.* - Merriam-Webster Dictionary

I PULLED MY restored, black, '78 Firebird through the open wrought iron gate past the stout brick pillars and up a crushed gravel circular drive. Finally, I parked at the top of the rise in front of a columned Georgian-style house—a red brick version of Tara, Scarlett O'Hara's plantation mansion in *Gone with the Wind*. Wide, New York bluestone steps led to a front entryway framed by trimmed shrubs, flowerbeds full of purple clematis, marsh marigolds and red tulips, and twin evergreens sculpted in loopy spiraling patterns. Redwood mulch covered the flowerbeds, filling the warm summer air with a fresh-cut wood scent.

Not your usual stomping grounds, is it, Gracie.

I rang the doorbell, tucked an errant lock of hair behind my ear, and waited, wondering what it must be like to grow up in Bexley—arguably one of the most affluent suburbs in Columbus—and here in Bullitt Park, specifically, an exclusive enclave of large mansions and grand estates, home to the crème of Ohio's elite.

A woman well into her forties, waging a war against that fact, answered the door dressed in tennis whites. *Of course.* Her frizzy, unruly hair was tied in a thick, straggly ponytail draped over her shoulder like a length of rope. She wore a white headband, blue-trimmed white wristbands, and full black-eyed makeup. The perky outfit and all the makeup in the world couldn't mask her bloodshot eyes and the smear of tears on her flushed cheeks.

"May I help you?"

"My name is Grace deHaviland." I handed her a business card. "Are you Virginia Beckman?"

"Yes."

"I'm a bail enforcement agent." I held up my badge and PI license. "Your attorney should have told you I'd be stopping by."

"Oh, yes. He did." She stepped back. "Please. Come in. Call me Ginny–everybody does." She forced a smile but wasn't able to hold it long.

"I've been hired to find Rebecca Weiss," I explained. "As you probably know, she jumped bail."

Ginny nodded.

"I'd like to ask your son, Chad, a few questions."

"Chad?" Ginny blinked, looking stunned. "Then you haven't heard?"

A voice boomed from somewhere inside the house. "Ginny! Whoever it is, tell 'em to get the hell out. We're busy here."

Ginny patted at her hair, and her gaze dropped to the floor. "I'm sorry, Grace. That's my husband, Tony. Maybe you'd better speak with him."

She ushered me into the wide, three-story-high foyer and shut the door behind me. White-trimmed archways on either side led to a labyrinth of doorways down halls so long they appeared endless. A sweeping staircase rose from near the front door to a second-floor landing, then continued to the third level. A white, high-gloss, chair-rail molding rimmed the foyer, with white, ornate panels below and beautiful, floral-patterned wallpaper above. Pink marble tile lay under my feet. I commented on how beautiful the floor was.

"Rosa aurora," Ginny said proudly.

It sounded impressive, so I nodded. To be polite.

A man appeared at the archway under the sweeping stairs. He was short, thick, and solidly built, roughly the dimensions of a fire hydrant, with a crew cut of iron-gray hair. He wore a well-tailored, powder blue dress shirt with the sleeves rolled two turns up his thick forearms and charcoal gray slacks. The shirt strained to contain his arms and broad chest, solid from a lifetime of heavy physical labor. Not the sort of man you'd imagine living in this kind of luxury.

"Goddamn it, Ginny, what are you lollygagging around out here for? We've—"

"Tony," she interrupted meekly. "This is Ms. deHaviland. The bounty hunter Charles told us about."

Tony Beckman's steel-gray eyes matched his steel-gray buzz cut. He arched a thick eyebrow and tugged at the knot of his silk tie with a thick finger. In his opposite hand, he held a beer in a can.

"The bounty hunter, hey." We shook hands. His was the size of a catcher's mitt: rough, blistered, and crushing.

"Hi, Grace." The voice came out from behind Beckman. A voice as familiar to me as it was unexpected.

"Suzie?" Suzie Jensen was a deputy sheriff and my best friend. "What are you doing here?"

"Wait," Beckman said. "You two know each other?"

"We've worked together before," Suzie said.

There was an understatement if ever I'd heard one. We'd gone to high school together. Joined the Sheriff's Department together. We were patrol partners for almost two years. Before I got myself fired. Over the years, she'd worked with me on dozens of cases, and I'd even helped her with a few of her police investigations.

"I should have known Louie'd call you in on this one," she said.

Louie Gravelle had put up the bond for Rebecca Weiss. With her bail at two-hundred-and-fifty-thousand dollars, he wouldn't lose that kind of loot without a fight, so he'd called me.

"I was the arresting officer," Suzie said. "When I heard Weiss didn't show up for court this afternoon, I had a patrol unit drop me off after work. To see how everyone was holding up."

That explained the civilian clothes, conservative for her: gray cargo pants, high-top sneakers, and a low-cut black tee-shirt under a denim jacket, minus her usual ear, nose, and eyebrow rings.

"But the boy, Chad," I said. "He's gone missing?"

Suzie nodded. "Since the Beckmans left court," she read from a notepad, "about 3:40 this afternoon."

I glanced at Mrs. Beckman in her tennis whites.

She must have read something in my face. Saw judgment in my expression. Or maybe she just felt guilty about not keeping better tabs on her son. "I had no idea Chad was gone. After they sent us home from court, he went straight to his room."

"Just like he always does," Tony Beckman said, sucking down the last drop of beer from his can. I waited for him to crush the aluminum in his fist, but he didn't.

"There was nothing more for us to do, so yes, I went to the club," Ginny continued. "I'm allowed that, aren't I?" She glanced at her husband like one might inspect a hornet's nest.

"Better than moping around here," Tony Beckman agreed. "And before you ask, yeah, I went to the office. I've lost enough time with all this crap." He shook the beer can. It was still empty. "And now this."

"When *did* you discover your son was gone?" I tried to keep my tone flat. God forbid I make it sound like an accusation.

"When Deputy Jensen arrived. I called Chad to come down. He didn't answer."

I asked Suzie, "You think he's hooked up with the woman again?"

She nodded. Her expression conveyed a sense of sadness and concern.

"Do we know if there's been any contact between them?"

Beckman pressed his lips into a frown so hard his upper lip puffed out. He hadn't a clue. I bet that applied to many things that went on at home. "I can't tell you the first thing about what that boy does. How the hell he thinks. Who could?"

"Until now, we've had no indication that they've spoken," Suzie said. "But I'm sure they're back together. She's behind this. She has to be."

"Do you have any idea where he might have gone?" I asked.

"No idea," Tony Beckman said, adding, "stupid-ass kid."

"What about you, Mrs. Beckman. A friend or a favorite relative? Places he likes to hang out?"

Tony Beckman didn't allow his wife to speak, answering for her. "The kid didn't have any friends," Beckman said. "He just stayed locked in his room all day playing computer games and chatting online, to God only knows who."

I was about to ask if we could look at Chad's computer or if he had a cell phone, but Ginny Beckman suddenly blurted out, "Brendon Parker. He's Chad's best friend. At least he was. Until all this happened. They had a falling out afterward…."

"Over his relationship with Rebecca Weiss?" I asked.

"I think so. Chad never said, but—"

Beckman interrupted. "Yeah, I remember him. He's that skinny dweeb with thick, black glasses. He did try to talk some sense into Chad, as scary a thought as that is."

Ginny spoke up. Her voice was so small I barely heard it. "He's a good kid, Tony. Really smart. He was Chad's best friend."

"Only one," Beckman grunted and left the foyer. I figured he'd remained dry for as long as he could stand. No doubt he was heading for the kitchen to get another beer. Or maybe something stronger.

Ginny gave us Brendon Parker's address, and Suzie wrote it in her notebook. I thanked Ginny. Suzie told her to stay by the phone in case Chad called. We'd be in touch. Tony Beckman didn't return to see us out.

OUTSIDE, I TOOK a deep, cleansing breath. The atmosphere in the house had been cloying. Toxic. No wonder the kid had run away. Heading down those wide New York bluestone steps in the fading summer sun, I didn't wonder about what it would be like to live there anymore. I'd gotten a glimpse. It made me ill just thinking about it.

"Mind giving me a lift?" Suzie asked. "Patrol dropped me off here after my shift."

I pulled the car door open. She slid in. Driving away from the mansion, I was glad for the opportunity to talk to Suzie. She could fill me in on the details. Give me the stuff I couldn't get from the arrest reports and the court papers.

The late afternoon sun dipped low behind a ribbon of purple-gray clouds strung wide across the horizon, infusing them with red and orange highlights, turning the sky a rich maroon. As if God had hit a dimmer switch on the day.

"Tell me about them," I said.

Suzie shrugged. "You know, your typical, rich, suburban family. Dad's a workaholic. Mom's the country club wife. They spend their days making money or spending it. Leaves no time for their kid. The old man, he came from nothing. A high school dropout. He worked as a day laborer for a construction company, sweeping floors and humping lumber. His words. Over the years, he went about learning the business. Worked his way up until, eventually, he took over the company. He now owns one of the largest construction firms in Ohio."

"Beckman Construction." I hadn't made the connection before. Their trucks were everywhere.

Suzie rubbed her thumb and forefinger together. "Big bucks."

Dad probably worked all day, every day, including weekends. Even when he was home, he probably fixed himself a drink, ate dinner, then it was off to a home office where he worked some more, making himself completely unavailable to his kid. And probably his wife, too.

While Ginny, with money to burn and time on her hands, went about the business of ingratiating themselves into the upper echelon of Columbus' high society, I guessed, by doing charity work and having lunch with the ladies. She played tennis and bridge and hosted the monthly book club in their home when she wasn't organizing the latest fundraiser, leaving Chad to be brought up by nannies, the maids, and his tutors. Giving him everything he wanted, everything he asked for, except the one thing he needed: their love and attention.

"You seem to know a lot about this kid," I said.

"I told you. I arrested Rebecca Weiss." Her reply was curt, warning me she didn't want to discuss it.

So, of course, I pressed her. "And?"

Chad's best friend, Brendon Parker, lived in Whitehall, a neighborhood bordering Bexley to the west. As we drove along East Broad Street, Suzie stared out the side window, watching the strip malls, gas stations, and chain restaurants pass. When she finally turned to look at me, her expression was full of anger and resentment. I didn't know why.

"After we arrested Rebecca Weiss and the full story started coming out, I conducted the victim impact interviews. Chad and I connected then. He opened up to me about what'd happened. About his life. About his parents. He's a good kid, Grace. One who's starved for attention. It's no wonder Weiss got her hooks into him. There. Happy?"

She pointed out the window to the left. "We're here."

Brendon Parker lived in a small community of tract homes off East Broad Street. The houses were carbon copies of one another: small, cookie-cutter ranches with clapboard siding and asphalt shingle roofs. Some were beige, some were white, and some were a God-awful bright blue. Yet the neighborhood wasn't a disgrace. The fifty-by-fifty-foot lots were neatly mowed and well-maintained, filling the air with the smell of fresh-cut grass. Cars sat out in driveways and lined the curbs, but they weren't junkers. Like the bikes and balls and other summertime toys littering the yards, they gave the neighborhood a community feel. Casual and welcoming.

Brendon's house was one of the blue ones. An air conditioning unit jutted out from what looked like a bedroom window. It rattled noisily. The front door was open, but the storm door wasn't.

I rang the doorbell. It bonged, muted behind the glass-and-metal storm door.

"Who is it?" a woman shouted from the back of the house, but it was a thin, young man with black-rimmed glasses and oily black hair, wearing a *Battlestar Galactica* tee-shirt, who appeared at the door.

"I've got it, Mom!" To us, he said, "Can I help you?"

Suzie badged him. She said, "Sheriff's Department."

"Shit. Cops. This is about Chad, isn't it?"

"Yes," Suzie said. "Why do you say it like that?"

His face soured, but he swung open the storm door. "'Cause it's always about Chad."

"Who is it, dear?" The woman's voice called out over the sound of metal bowls clanging in the rear of the house. I smelled fresh-baked cookies. The aroma made my stomach growl, reminding me that I'd missed lunch.

"Cops, Mom. They wanna talk to me. Again."

The front door opened directly into a neat but dated living room. Wood paneling covered the walls. A worn couch sat under the picture window and two overstuffed chairs with a small table between them faced a dark brick mantle. The hearth was black and sooty, suggesting it was well-used, with coal-tipped fireplace tools in a brass stand nearby. I imagined a family gathered around the warmth of a fire, cozy during cold winter nights.

This was a world far removed from the stiff, formal ambiance of Bullitt Park and the Beckman mansion. I wondered how Brendon and Chad knew each other. How they became friends.

Suzie said, "Have you seen or heard from Chad recently?"

Brendon shook his head.

I glanced at Suzie. She nodded, giving me the go-ahead. "Rebecca Weiss walked out of court today and didn't come back. Chad's parents have reported him missing. Do you think the two of them are together?"

"Well, duh!"

I'm told that's the way kids talk these days. That they're not necessarily being disrespectful. Maybe so, but if he didn't get a civil tongue in his head, I was going to rip it out. "You've no idea where the two of them might have gone?"

He eyed me, wary of my sudden sharp tone. Good. "No. Chad and me. We don't hang out anymore. Not since, you know, all this shit started."

"You mean Rebecca Weiss."

"Yeah, that." He shook his head. "It got crazy. Too crazy."

Well, Duh! I thought, wondering how else you would describe a fifteen-year-old kid having a year-long sexual affair with his twenty-three-year-old teacher; her being arrested on multiple statutory rape charges, among other things; and Chad being remanded to mandatory therapy sessions. Yeah, pretty crazy.

Brendon's mother appeared at the opening between the living room and dining room, a plate of chocolate chip cookies on the dining room table behind her. She wiped her hands on an apron coated with flour and came over, introducing herself, "Amanda Parker. How can we help you?"

"We're looking for Chad Beckman," Suzie said. "We believe he's in the company of Rebecca Weiss."

Mom clucked. "That woman. Imagine. All the trouble she's caused."

"We were hoping Brendon might know where they are."

"Son?"

He shrugged. "I don't know where they are."

"Are you sure?"

"Mom!" Like how dare she not believe her fifteen-year-old son? What was she thinking? "I don't talk to Chad anymore. He's weird now. Creeps me out."

I let Suzie run with that one.

"We heard you, and he were tight," Suzie said.

"Used to be, yeah," Brendon said defensively. "He's a freak show now. I don't want anything to do with him."

"Fine." Suzie's tone was sharp. Her patience was wearing thin. "But do you have any idea where he is?"

"Geez. Aren't you listening, lady? I don't talk to him. I don't see him. I don't know."

I could tell the kid was starting to tick Suzie off. That didn't happen often, but when it did, watch out, things usually got crazy. Luckily, Mrs. Parker stepped forward. "Chad, please. If you know anything, you need to tell them."

"Goddamn it, Mom, I told you. I don't know. Why won't you ever listen to me?"

Mrs. Parker didn't get a chance to answer because Suzie suddenly pushed between mother and son and grabbed Brendon by the shirt, balling it up in her fists and pulling him close. Nose to nose, she said, "This isn't about you, you little shit. You knew about Chad and Rebecca Weiss from the start, right?"

Shocked, Mrs. Parker said, "Officer. Please."

Brendon licked his lips. "Yeah. Yes."

Suzie narrowed her blue eyes. "Has he contacted you?"

"No. I swear. I told you! I stopped talking to him."

"But you know something," I guessed, speaking over Suzie's shoulder.

"No, I don't," he insisted.

He might not have been lying, but he did know more than he was saying. You interview enough people—witnesses, victims, and suspects—you get a feel. The way they stand, the way they make eye contact. Or don't. It tells you things. It told me Brendon was holding something back.

"Out with it, Brendon," Suzie gave him a shake. "What aren't you telling us?"

"Officer. I must insist…." Mrs. Parker placed a hand on Suzie's shoulder.

"Nothing," Brendon said. "I swear."

"Suzie," I warned. Things were getting out of hand, and I wasn't quite sure why.

Suzie tightened her grip on his shirt and shook him. Hard. "Tell me where he is. Tell me!"

Mrs. Parker gasped. I stepped forward, angling between her and Suzie, putting a hand on Suzie's arm and signaling Mrs. Parker to back off. "Easy."

"Okay, okay," Brendon cried out. "Look. I don't know anything, but I think…."

"Go on," Suzie said.

"Let go of my son, officer. Or I'm calling 911."

Suzie glanced anger-filled daggers at Mrs. Parker, but she released her grip on Brendon and stepped back. His mom put an arm around his shoulders and pulled him toward her. "I think you both had better go."

"Tell us what you know, Brendon," I said. "For Chad's sake."

Nervously, he gazed at Suzie and pushed his black-rimmed glasses up his narrow nose. "Okay. Okay. Like I said, I don't know, but I think … I never un-friended Chad on Facebook. Today, he changed his status. Now it reads something like, 'Our plans are finally working out. In a few hours, we'll be together. We'll start our new life away from here, forever.' Something like that, I don't remember the exact words."

Our plans. We'll be together. Away from here, forever.

Suzie asked, "Do you know what that means? Where they would go?"

"Anything you can think of will help," I said, "Anything at all."

"Wait. I do remember something. Chad used to talk a lot about going to Mexico. Maybe they went there."

No, I thought. Rebecca Weiss had surrendered her passport as a condition of her bail. The arrest warrant made it impossible for her to board a plane. Flying was out of the question. She could drive to the border, but from Columbus, that would take them days. Too long, too many chances to get stopped. No, not Mexico.

"Canada," I said. "They could reach the border in a few hours. And it's an easier crossing to make than Mexico, especially leaving the U.S. If they made it into Canada. From there, they could go anywhere."

They needed to get together first. And I had an idea.

"Brendon, where did Rebecca and Chad first hook up? As a couple? Did they have a special place? Someplace that held a particular meaning for them?"

The boy thought hard for a moment. I could tell because his forehead wrinkled and his eyes got narrow. When the epiphany hit, he looked up surprised, wide-eyed, and grinning. "Yeah. Sure. Chad talked about it all the time. The zoo. It was the first time they kissed and…" he looked at his mom and blushed. "And you know…."

"The zoo?" Suzie said. "The Columbus Zoo?"

"Yeah. He kept saying it was their special place."

THE COLUMBUS ZOO—five hundred acres, six-thousand animals, and eight world regions—a venue visited by one-and-a-half-million people each year. That's forty-one hundred people a day. All we had to do was find two of them. If they were even there in the first place. A piece of cake.

I pulled the Firebird through the parking entrance of the zoo. Suzie badged us past the parking attendant, and I pulled to the curb in front of the park gates. A uniformed guard approached us at a trot, quick to tell us we were in a pick-up and drop-off zone. We couldn't leave the car parked there.

Suzie was just as quick to tell him we were on the job. "Official business."

"Okay, sure." Eager to please, he said, "Anything I can do to help?"

"What time does the zoo close," I asked.

"Tonight? Nine o'clock."

The sun hung stubbornly over the tree-lined horizon, reluctant to give up its claim to the day. I checked my phone. A couple of hours. Regardless, in another hour, it would be dark. I waved at the turnstile openings. "Is this the only exit here?"

"For regular visitors, sure. We do have others, but they're only used in case of emergency. Is this?"

Suzie waved a dismissive hand. "No, nothing like that. We're looking for someone we think might be in the park."

The guard tipped his hat back and scratched his forehead. "Anyone dangerous?"

"No. We don't believe so."

That seemed to disappoint him. "Then yeah, best thing to do is to wait here for them to come out. Anything else I can help you with?"

"No," Suzie said. "Thanks. I think we've got it."

"You betcha." The guard moved off reluctantly, clearly not happy there wasn't something more he could do.

Don't give up hope, chico, I thought. Whenever Suzie and I worked together, things got…exciting.

I pushed my seat back a little and settled in, getting comfortable. Surveillance had never been my strong suit. Sitting around and doing nothing simply chafed me. I preferred to be on the go, moving, tracking, hunting down those I'm going after. But sometimes, patience was the only way to go. "So, I guess we just sit here and wait."

"Guess so." Suzie sat forward, looking past me, scrutinizing each visitor who exited the park. Luckily, the crowd was light. Without too much trouble, we kept up with the flow of people leaving the zoo.

I gave it a few minutes, then said, "You want to talk about what happened back there?"

"What? At Parker's house? That was nothing."

"Don't nothing me, Suzie. You were about to tune that boy up. And in front of his mother. What's up with that?"

"He was being a jerk."

I agreed, but I knew Suzie, and there was more to it than that. "Ever since we left the Beckman's, you've been in a mood."

"Have not." She looked around me, intensely watching a woman with long auburn hair tied in a ponytail and pulled through the back of a yellow baseball cap. The woman was alone, wearing shorts and carrying a large canvas tote bag. I had Rebecca Weiss's mug shot and several other pictures of her from the newspapers and TV indelibly imprinted in my brain. Other than the auburn hair, this woman didn't come anywhere close. Suzie shook her head, arriving at the same conclusion, and leaned back.

"Come on, Suzie. What is it about this case that's eating at you?"

"I told you. I interviewed the kid. Chad. I spent a lot of time with him. He's young and confused, impressionable. Being with that woman…that family of his, it's messed him up. I can't stand seeing anybody messed up like that."

Tony Beckman was a rough number. In some ways, he reminded me of Suzie's dad. A man without Beckman's money but with the same blue-collar roots. That same *only the strong deserve to survive* attitude. Suzie hated her dad and, to my knowledge, hadn't seen him in the last ten years, even though he still lived in Reynoldsburg, ten minutes from her condo in Columbus. Did she see the similarities? Was that what bonded her to this kid? Or was there more?

"Aren't you overstating the case just a little bit?" I asked.

She shifted in her seat to face me, her icy blue eyes flared with anger. "No, Grace. I'm not. Have you any idea what's going on here? The danger the boy is in."

I didn't mean to be cavalier about it, but I shrugged. "Not really. I'm not exactly seeing Bonnie and Clyde here, Suzie. More like a skeevy Romeo and Juliet."

"Romeo and Juliet? You're not serious? Grace. She's twenty-three years old. He's sixteen. Fifteen when this whole thing started. It's disgusting."

"Did you miss the part where I said skeevy?"

I got the whole statutory rape thing. How a teacher exploited her authority over a vulnerable young boy. I understood how pathetic that made them both, how desperate or lonely or just plain fucked up. I got all that. What I didn't get was Suzie's reaction. Why was she so worked up over it?

Maybe it was me, but Suzie had dealt with rapists and junkies and abusers her whole professional life—the worst humanity could produce—and she did it without getting as agitated as she was now. Cops get called out to all kinds of vile situations. They can't afford to get emotionally vested in every case they work, or it'll tear them apart. Suzie knew that. And, normally, she was as good at remaining emotionally detached as anybody. What was it about this investigation? Why did it affect her like this?

"Look," I said, trying to smooth things over. "I'm not condoning what she did. It's debased and manipulative. An abuse of her authority over a pathetic, needy teenager, but we're talking about a kid who scored with his teacher."

"Are you kidding me, Grace?" The appalled look I got came as a surprise. "Let me ask you something. Would you be so 'it's no big deal' if Chad were an underage girl and Rebecca Weiss was a man?"

Suzie arched an eyebrow, waiting. I didn't answer. Did gender change anything? Should it?

My silence confirmed her point, mollifying her, but she remained upset with me. "Yeah, I thought so. He's too young for all this deviant shit, Grace. He can't handle it. That's why there're laws against this kind of thing. That's why it's wrong." Frustrated, she added, "I've talked to this boy, Grace. A lot. This thing has scrambled the kid's head. He can't sleep. He's begun to drink. He's even cutting himself. Up and down his arms. I'm afraid he might really hurt himself if he doesn't get the help he needs."

I didn't know what to say to that. I didn't say anything.

We sat in silence. I thought about everything she'd said. Okay, so maybe it was more complicated than I'd first thought. It was about more than simply sex and a kid crushing on his teacher, getting that common fantasy fulfilled. It was about trust and feelings, and needs. About a predator taking advantage of someone weak. Vulnerable and susceptible to the charm and the lies and the abuse.

After leaving me alone with my own thoughts for way too long, Suzie said quietly, "There they are."

I checked out the stream of people leaving the zoo. Rebecca Weiss wore a pair of oversized dark sunglasses, even though the sun had set an hour before. She had on a wide floppy-brim hat, a scarf wrapped around her face, and a trench coat belted tightly around her waist. She looked like the tabloid's latest favorite celeb trying to hide from the paparazzi. Not so surprising, considering she was a wanted woman. Not to mention the sensationalized coverage this case had received.

The sky had darkened to a deep purpling black now that the sun had dropped behind the thatch roofs of the zoo's outside concession stands, casting long, dark shadows across the walkway and stretching into the parking lot where the security lights failed to reach.

With Rebecca Weiss was a young man—a kid, really. He wore a light jacket, his stringy brown hair overly long. He had gangly arms and legs, with feet too large for the rest of him, as if he hadn't grown into them yet.

"Okay," I said. "You know these two. How do you want to play this?"

Suzie pulled her Lady Smith—the girly revolver she carried off-duty—and concealed it in the pocket of her jacket. "Weiss is desperate. Jumping bail means she'll probably not come easily. Add to that, she's an out-and-out bitch."

"Okay. But…."

"Just needed saying," Suzie told me, opening her door. "They don't know you. You can get close without spooking them. You make the approach. When you do, I'll grab Chad. You take Weiss."

"The out-and-out bitch that won't come easily," I said. "Great." I did nothing to tamper down the sarcasm in my voice.

Rebecca Weiss and Chad were holding hands, walking along with a crowd streaming briskly into the parking lot and diverging down the various aisles of parked cars. The throng was a mix of adults and kids, the younger ones hopping up and down: skipping and talking excitedly; their balloons bopping up in the air. Their arms loaded with stuffed animals, bags of popcorn and ice cream and cotton candy, and cheap animal toys.

I weaved through the horde. Like a racehorse threading its way to the middle of the pack. Closing the gap between my targets and me. I felt Suzie behind me, staying close and using me to hide in case Rebecca or Chad glanced back before we could grab the two of them.

When I felt the timing was right, I gave Suzie a quick glance.

She nodded back, ready as well.

I was an arm's length away from Rebecca Weiss. I called out, "Ms. Weiss."

She twisted around to see who'd called her. An involuntary response. Annoyance lines creased the visible swath of skin between her oversized sunglasses and the big-brim, floppy hat.

I grabbed her arm.

She cried out. "Hey!"

Chad spun at the commotion. He locked eyes on Suzie. "Becca! It's the cops!"

Rebecca tried to pull away, but I held onto her arm and snapped a handcuff around her wrist. She struggled against my efforts to grab her other arm.

Chad shouted. "Stop! Leave her alone!" To the crowd, he screamed, "This woman's attacking us! Help!"

Suzie held her badge high over her head. "Police! No one interfere! Chad, stop this."

I yanked the cuff I had secured around Rebecca's wrist. She yelped in pain and reached for her wrist with her free hand. As I'd hoped. I caught her forearm and twisted it up behind her back. She cursed while I got her cuffed without too much trouble.

"Who are you?" she shouted. "Let me go!"

"Grace deHaviland," I said. "Bail enforcement. Quit struggling—you'll only hurt yourself."

Rebecca Weiss didn't listen and continued to thrash about. Fear made her strong, but not strong enough. I held her in an effective arm lock. It didn't take her long to realize she wasn't getting away from me. When reality struck—or maybe she just became too tired to fight anymore—she went slack in my grip.

As far as takedowns go, this one had gone amazingly well.

Chad Beckman was a different story.

"No! Stop it! Let. Her. Go."

As strong and scrappy as Suzie was, she had trouble keeping hold of the wiry kid. He hopped up and down as though he had springs in his shoes. She pulled on his arm, tried to anchor him, to keep him away from Rebecca, away from interfering with me.

He yanked his arm, frantic to escape from Suzie's grasp, but she held firm. I thought he might try to slug her with his free hand—and that would've been a bad mistake. Lucky for him, he didn't try. "You don't understand. I *want* to be with her. We belong together."

"No, Chad. You don't," Suzie yelled. "We've talked about this. It feels that way now. Trust me. I know." Suzie jerked his arm. "Look at me."

He did, and standing quietly with the woman who'd caused all this grief, I saw his eyes fill with tears. They clung to his eyelashes momentarily, then flowed down his face. His mouth opened and closed and he made little mewing sounds, but he looked at Suzie. She touched his neck and guided his face into her shoulder. His gasping sobs became muffled by the worn denim of her jacket.

I took that as my cue and tugged on Rebecca's arm. "Let's go."

The crowd around us started to break up at the urging of the arriving security force. They pushed people back. Moved them along. The guard who'd stopped us when we first arrived made an opening in the crowd for me. I steered Rebecca Weiss through it, heading back toward the zoo entrance. To Suzie, I mouthed the word *car*.

She nodded over Chad's bawling—*okay.*

AT MY CAR, I put a call into my old boss, chief deputy of patrol James Lee Tolman. I filled him in on our situation. He agreed to send a patrol unit right over. Seven minutes later, a cruiser pulled into the lot with lights flashing but no sirens. Two young deputies I didn't know got out and took the bail papers I offered them: my authorization to apprehend Rebecca Weiss. One deputy looked over the papers while the other put Rebecca into the back seat of the cruiser.

I told them I'd be down to the station shortly to process the paperwork. Once they were gone, and while I waited for Suzie to finish consoling a very distraught Chad Beckman, I called Louie Gravelle, the bail bondsman who'd put up Rebecca Weiss's bail. I told him she was in custody. Then I told him to write me a check.

Chad looked miserable when Suzie finally brought him over to the car. Suzie didn't look much better, either.

I opened the passenger side door and pulled forward the seat. Chad climbed into the back for the drive to Bexley, an awkward, oppressively silent trip. Often, I glanced in the rearview mirror. Chad sat sniffing, rubbing his nose with the sleeve of his jacket. Tears streaked his face. I guessed Suzie had been right. He was just a kid. A kid horribly exploited by his teacher, by someone responsible for taking care of him, not hurting him.

At the Beckman mansion, I waited outside while Suzie took Chad back to his parents. I sat, left alone with nothing but my thoughts and the gathering darkness. It made for a very long hour. When Suzie climbed into the car, she looked wrung out.

"You okay?" I asked.

"No," she said. "Let's go."

I didn't. I turned to her instead. "I've been thinking. Back there at the zoo, you said something. You told Chad, 'Trust me, I know.' Know what?"

"I was just talking him down."

"No. You weren't." I pointed at the Beckman mansion. "There's something about this case that's got you all twisted. What is it?"

"Nothing," she said. "Come on, just drive."

"Not until you talk to me." Mom was a hot-tempered Latina, and my dad was a stubborn-as-they-come Mick. For better or worse, I'd inherited both hard-assed qualities in spades. I would sit there until hell froze over, and Suzie knew it.

"Talk to you about what?"

"Why is this case tearing you up like this? Hell, Suzie, we've known each other since high school. I can tell when something's eating at you. Something's wrong. Spill, girl."

"All right. You're so smart. Fine." She shifted in her seat, turning away from me to stare out the window at the topiary in the yard. "You think this is some kind of victimless crime. A kid who scored with his teacher. No big deal. But you have no idea how messed up that kid is right now. He's confused, and he's hurt. He's got no one to turn to, no one to talk to. Part of him thinks he's in love with her. The other part knows it's wrong, that he's been abused." She spoke to me but kept looking out the passenger window. "Inside him, those opposing sides are kicking his ass. He needs help."

"Suzie, I was wrong. Seeing Chad that way, I realize that now."

She cut me off. "Grace, don't patronize me. You don't know what you're talking about."

That lit my Latina temper. "Damn it, Suzie. I'm trying to understand."

She snapped her head around. The torment etched on her face scared me. "But you never will. You can't. Not unless it's happened to you."

Stunned, like the slow kid in the back of the class, I said, "What are you telling me?" This was a woman I'd known for years. We've partied together. We've saved each other's lives. She told me everything—or so I'd thought.

Suzie stared down at her hands. She held them in her lap, one over the other. Then she looked away, her chin quivering. "Sophomore year in high school. Do you remember Arlene Moore?"

I'd first met Suzie in our sophomore year, but I didn't know her well just then; we didn't become tight until the following year—when we were juniors. High school held few good memories for me. I didn't try to dredge them up very often. Now, for my friend, I dug deep. "She was the art teacher, right?"

Suzie nodded. She had been quite the sketch artist when we first met. She drew and painted really good stuff, I always thought, but then she just stopped. It only now dawned on me that she'd stopped around that time and never drew or painted anything after that. I'd never thought to ask her why.

"Arlene Moore molested me." Suzie swallowed hard. "I didn't think of it like that back when it was happening. I thought she liked me. She said I was special."

I put a hand on her arm. "When? How?"

"I had her for art class. She took an interest in me. Told me my stuff was really good. She told me she could help me with my drawing. Soon she started having me come to her classroom after school for special lessons. At first, we'd sit and talk, and I'd draw. She'd give me pointers. It was so wonderful to have someone to talk to, someone who would listen to me, hear me, and act as though I had something worthwhile to say. I really liked her. She didn't treat me like some stupid kid."

My throat tightened up. Silently, I listened. My hands clenched in tight fists. I'd known Suzie then, but I had no idea. She never told me.

"It started on one of our 'personal field trips.' After school and on weekends, she'd take me to art shows and museums and stuff. She told me I should call her Arlene. She wasn't my teacher when we weren't in school, she said. She told me to think of her as a friend or a big sister."

An only child, Suzie had a home life that was the pits. She and Sam, her ultra-conservative, emotionally stunted father, had no relationship except as sparring partners. Their situation was made worse by Sam's inability to cope with Suzie's increasingly alcoholic mother. The more the woman slipped into the bottle, the more time Sam spent away from the house. I guess he hoped the whole miserable situation would all just disappear.

It did. Suzie's mom died from the disease, and Sam lost his daughter.

"The first time was late winter, the end of February," Suzie said. "We were at an exhibition at the Franklin Conservatory. I commented on how beautiful a Gauguin was. She said it was as beautiful as me. Then she kissed me.

"I freaked. But she took me in her arms. Told me how much she liked me and that it was okay for women to be together like that. How there really wasn't that much difference in our ages. And she wouldn't be my teacher forever."

Suzie shook her head. "I didn't know what to do. Part of me wanted to run away, but I was afraid. Afraid she'd be mad at me. Afraid she'd tell my parents. I didn't want to hurt her feelings. I didn't want her to be mad at me. Oh, God, Grace, I *wanted* to be with her. Alone. She took me to her apartment..."

Suzie's voice cracked. She couldn't go on.

She didn't need to. The picture was clear. "How long did this go on?" I asked, in as neutral a voice as I could.

"The rest of the school year. Until the summer."

"Suzie. We were friends by then. Why didn't you tell me?"

My throat was tight and dry.

She shrugged. "She told me I couldn't tell anyone. It had to be our little secret. I knew it was wrong, but part of me didn't care. I just wanted to be wanted, you know?" She wiped at a tear that fell down her face. "I was so confused. Sexually. Emotionally. It felt bad. It felt wrong. But to have someone who cared about me. Someone who liked me. I didn't want to lose that either."

She shook her head. "You and I weren't good enough friends, Grace. Not then. Not to share something like that."

I worked hard to keep the hurt from my retort. "But afterward…."

"It was over. I was … ashamed. What would be the point?"

"Why did it stop?" Thinking back, I remembered Arlene Moore hadn't returned to teach the following year, our junior year. "Did someone find out?"

"I don't know. I never knew. She was just gone after that, moved away without a word. I'd heard rumors of another girl, of several other girls, in fact." Suzie snorted. "So much for my being special to her."

Her eyes glistened, wet with tears, and reflected the lights bathing the Beckman mansion in a white glow. "I was so messed up by that time. I didn't know who I was. What I was. I was so glad when it was over. Afraid of it and tired of lying, so scared someone would find out. But I was angry too. I felt abandoned. And I couldn't help wondering, had she really liked me or had she just been using me?"

Suzie gave a short laugh. "If you remember, I went a little crazy that summer."

"You cut your hair."

She'd had long, natural, blond hair down to her waist when I'd met her. Every day, she came to school with a different hairstyle: wavy and thick one day; flat iron straight the next; in a ponytail or pigtails or piled up in a bun after that. That summer, she'd cut all that beautiful hair off. I remembered. It was as if she'd hacked it off with hedge clippers and without the benefit of a mirror.

Her father, Sam, said she looked like a dyke. Her mom barely noticed—she just drank more.

"I wish you'd told me," I said then.

"What would you have done, Grace? What could you have done?"

I didn't have an answer for that.

Suzie reached out and cupped my hand. "Through all my craziness, all my stupid stunts, you did the one thing I needed you to do. You became my friend."

I didn't know what to say in response. If she thought I'd been there for her, I was glad, though I couldn't imagine how she thought so. I couldn't recall doing anything to earn her gratitude. I had so much of my own shit to deal with in those days the only thing I could remember was my own adolescent, self-destructive insanity.

If I'd helped her, that made me happy. And gave me hope. Maybe I wasn't the self-absorbed, crazy, rebellious bitch I thought I was.

"I'm so sorry." I said, "Maybe we can—"

I stopped mid-sentence. The front door of the Beckman house ripped open, splashing a long rectangle of light across the expensive bluestone. Ginny Beckman ran down the steps. Barefoot, her robe flapping and her arms waving. "Thank God you're still here! Come quick! Come quick!"

Suzie threw open the car door and rolled out fast. I scrambled after her, sprinting around the front of the car. Ginny kept waving her hands in frantic windmill motions.

"What's wrong? What is it?" Suzie took the woman by the shoulders, trying to steady her. Hysterical didn't come close to describing Ginny Beckman at that moment.

She pawed at Suzie's jacket. "Upstairs! Quick. You have to do something. Please."

A quick glance passed between Suzie and me. No question we'd help. The question was: with what? We ran full out for the house, through the foyer and up the staircase. Ginny couldn't keep up with us. Suzie called down to her. "Where?"

"Upstairs," Ginny said. "Chad's room."

We reached the third floor, winded. Three flights of winding stairs at full tilt, pumped full of adrenaline, will do that to you. Even an avid runner like me.

Tony Beckman stood with his back against the door jamb. He was in the same dress shirt and slacks he'd had on earlier. A beer can lay on its side at his feet, its contents soaking into the carpet.

He barely reacted as we charged down the hall. His bulldog expression, now colorless and drained, never changed.

Suzie shouldered past him and entered the room first. I heard her breath catch in her throat as she stopped short. I barreled into her, doing my best not to knock her down.

"Oh my God."

Across the room, Chad hung from a belt. He'd tied one end to the closet doorknob: the other end cinched around his neck. His legs were splayed out, his body not quite reaching the floor. His arms lay akimbo. His head lolled to one side. His tongue hung from between his purple lips. His eyelids were half-shut.

Beside Chad lay a single sheet of lined, white paper torn from a small spiral notebook. It was all wrinkled up, as if he'd clutched it in his hand as he thrashed, gasping for breath, struggling until all his oxygen was gone. In death, his hand relaxed, and the paper had slipped to the floor.

Suzie squatted beside him. She felt for a pulse. When she looked up at me, she shook her head.

She picked up the paper, reading it once to herself, her lips silently moving. She read it again. This time, aloud, "I'm so confused. People won't leave us alone. They don't understand. I don't understand. All I know is I can't live without her. I love her."

Suzie stumbled into my arms and cried.

I held her tight and did the only thing I could: be there for her—now more than ever.

###

FAMILY MATTERS

"BAIL ENFORCEMENT AGENT? I do not know what this means."

She sat at a small Formica table in her cramped, dreary kitchen, with its old, chipped stove and tiny, humming refrigerator. The walls were grease spattered. The air was rich with chili powder, coriander, and cumin. She fingered the business card I'd handed her when she answered the front door.

Along with my occupation, it had my name: Grace deHaviland.

"It means I'm a bounty hunter, Mrs. Navarro."

"It means," she said. "You want to take my boy back to jail."

"Hector has done a very bad thing, Mrs. Navarro."

Maria Navarro put the card down on the table and slid it back to me. Rejecting it—and me—with the subtle gesture. She sat back. The cheap metal chair creaked. Its plastic padding expelled a puff of air, like a sigh.

"The police are looking for him, too," I reminded her. "It would be best if I found him first." I let her think about that while she tried to figure me out.

The cramped apartment was hot, trapping the early Indian summer air, stagnant and thick. A trickle of sweat rolled under my loose-fitting collar and down my spine.

Maria Navarro brushed a limp corkscrew of black hair from her forehead and sat forward again, her forearms on the table's edge. Younger than she looked, life had taken its toll on her. She took back my card.

"Why?" she asked. "Why would it be best for you to arrest my boy? For this thing he did not do? And not the *policia?* Either way, my Hector will be in jail."

"Because," I explained, "I want to bring Hector in alive. The police will be less concerned with that than I am." And why was that, one might ask. Because I can't collect a bounty on a dead man. Often, that's more the pity. I didn't tell Mrs. Navarro that, of course. That would've been insensitive. Not to mention counterproductive.

Hector Navarro had been arrested for assault and several lesser charges, all stemming from a beating he'd given Ramon Ruiz a few weeks ago. A beating so bad it put Ruiz in a coma. Though he'd faced violent felony charges, the judge in the case offered him bail anyway, which Hector made.

Since then, things had changed.

The most important development being Ramon Ruiz had died two days earlier. Hector had been ordered back to court to face amended charges. And no doubt bail revocation. And now, he was in the wind.

"You only wish to collect your bounty, Ms. deHaviland. I am not a stupid woman."

"No, ma'am, you're not," I agreed. "And I won't insult you by lying to you. I only get paid to bring your son in alive. That's true. It's my job. But my reasons don't matter. In the end, we both want the same thing. Hector safe."

A window fan whirled in a front room, doing little more than move the hot, midday, September air around. The Navarro apartment sat over a dry-cleaning store. The chemical smell mixed with the spicy kitchen scents, corrupting the memory such aromas conjured for me of my own Latina mother's

Sundays spent in the kitchen making shrimp ceviche, enchiladas, Spanish rice, and plantains con crema.

"But I tell you again, Ms. deHaviland. My boy did not do this terrible, terrible thing." She fisted her hands and pressed them between her ample breasts. "I know this in my heart."

I exhaled. "Whether he did or didn't isn't why I'm here. I don't investigate. I'm not the police. Nor do I decide his guilt or innocence. That is for a judge and jury to decide. My job is simply to find him and bring him in."

Her eyes filled with tears, shimmering and ready to fall, as I dashed any hopes she had I might be a sympathetic ear. I always hated this part, trying to convince people who know my skips to help me. Trying to convince them that it's in the skips' best interests that I bring them in. I'm an ex-cop, a bounty hunter for twelve-plus years. I know better, even if they don't.

"Please," she said as the tears fell, tracking down her doughy cheeks. "I can prove my Hector did not do this. I can." She snapped to her feet so fast her chair slid across the grimy floor and banged into the metal cabinets behind her.

I jumped despite myself. "Mrs. Navarro, please."

But her dark eyes had turned to iron. Her forehead furrowed under a curtain of limp black bangs. She brushed them back with a hand and a puff of hot breath. "You want my help to bring in my boy, to save him from the *policia*. I will help. But first, you must know the truth. I will not help unless you listen." She tapped her right ear with two extended fingers. "And truly hear."

"Okay, Mrs. Navarro," I said, standing up. If I had to endure her telling me what a good boy Hector was, her showing me gold star report cards he'd received in middle school or the cheap trophies he'd won in Little League when he was eight years old, to get the information I'd come for, fine. Besides, I felt sorry for her, this single mother, working to raise her young boy right, alone, in a pretty tough neighborhood. A hard thing to do. "I'll listen to what you have to say, Mrs. Navarro." I smiled. "And I will hear."

Maria Navarro flashed a grateful smile and took me by the hand.

"This way," she said but didn't lead me deeper into the apartment as I expected. No, she took me to the door next to the grease-coated stove and flung it open to the outside world.

Beyond the back door, we walked along a narrow, covered porch of wood, painted gray, with a white spindle railing. It ran the length of the building, linking the four apartments in both directions. At each apartment, a set of wooden stairs, also painted gray, led steeply to a back alley below. There, several banged-up, late-model cars sat parked on a poorly maintained macadam lot, including an old Charger up on milk crates.

At a back door three apartments down from hers, she stopped.

"Here," she said. "Ramon Ruiz's girlfriend lives here." She knocked loudly on the peeling wood doorframe. "Rosalina Calandria Lopez! It's Mrs. Navarro. Come out here, please."

"What do you want, woman?" called out an insolent, young Latina voice from the shadowy interior of the apartment. I looked through the window next to the door, into the kitchen. From what I could see, the layout appeared to be identical to that of Maria Navarro's apartment. "I told you I don't want to talk to you no more. What don't you understand?"

"I have someone here, Rosalina," Mrs. Navarro said. "Someone you need to tell about Hector, tell about what happened that night. She won't bring you harm." She looked at me. I nodded. I was only interested in information.

"Who is she?" A pretty Latina, full of youthful attitude and inner-city vigilance, appeared at the screen door. She gazed through the screen but kept the door latched. "What do you want?"

"I want to talk about that night," I said.

"You the police?"

"No."

The girl's bare shoulders—she wore a black tank top—dropped, just a fraction, but enough. Less combative, she asked again, "What do you want to know?"

I wasn't sure. Rosalina Lopez was Ramon Ruiz's girlfriend. She had been with Hector and Ramon the night they fought. She'd made a statement to police, told how Hector beat up Ramon, nearly killing him. It seemed unlikely this girl knew where Hector was now or would be willing to help me find him.

I also wondered, given the relationships at play here, why Mrs. Navarro would seek the help of Ruiz's girlfriend. This was, after all, Hector's accuser. More was going on than I could see at the moment.

"You're not any kind of cop?" she asked again, buying time while she decided what she should do.

Angry and impatient, Mrs. Navarro slapped the doorframe. "Tell her, Rosalina Lopez! Tell her what happened. Tell her how you lied to the police that night."

Two aluminum frame chairs sat outside under the kitchen window, the colorful fabric strips weather-beaten and torn. A clothesline on a pulley ran from the door frame to a pole, out to the fort-like fence separating the parking lot from the back of the deli lot next door. Several shirts and towels hung from the line, limp in the windless air. A couple of shirtless adolescent boys ran across the street, carrying a baseball bat and gloves.

I waited, but Rosalina remained mute, so I asked, "What lie did you tell to the police, Rosalina?"

Rosalina cast her gaze at her feet, her posture filled with shame. Or maybe it was fear. She fiddled with the door hook, then came out onto the gray porch. Mrs. Navarro and I stepped back to give her room, and the screen door slammed shut with a bang. Rosalina leaned against the closed door, her hands behind her back, her head still down.

We stood, waiting for Rosalina to work up the courage to tell her story.

"It's important you tell me what you know, Rosalina," I said.

Her head came up. She was a pretty girl in her late teens. Her tank top flaunted a taunt, flat belly over a pair of low-riding True Religion jeans. Her hair was shiny and black and tied into a small ponytail at the nape of her neck. She had dusky, flawless skin and eyes that were dark, sensual, and alert. They were bloodshot from crying.

"People call me Rosie."

I nodded and smiled. "Okay, Rosie. What happened?"

"Hector didn't beat up Ramon. He was Hector's friend."

"They grew up together. Here," Mrs. Navarro offered. "Two little *amigos* since the first grade."

According to the police report given to Large Louie, the bail bondsman I freelanced for, both boys worked at the Olive Garden restaurant up on Taylor Square Road in Reynoldsburg—the next town over from where they lived here in Whitehall. Hector worked in the kitchen, as a dishwasher mostly, but he helped prepare meals in a pinch, fixing the salads and dishing food onto plates. Ramon was a busboy.

The two young men had worked at the restaurant for the last six months and had no work-related issues. The fight occurred only a few blocks away at 1:30 in the morning.

"In your statement, you said you waited for their shift to end. They came out, and the three of you were walking to the bus stop, but Hector and Ramon had an argument. What about?"

"Rosalina," Mrs. Navarro said sharply. "Tell her."

116

Rosie flinched. "Okay, okay. There was no argument. Not between Hector and Ramon. It was with three other boys. Three college boys." She sneered. "Three drunk, white college boys."

There was no mention in the bail papers I'd received about anyone else being at the scene. "Tell me about these boys."

"They were white," she said, making that point clear. "And they wore football jerseys. OSU jerseys—Ohio State. They staggered, using up the whole sidewalk. We tried to stay out of their way, but one boy bumped into me as we passed. I think he did it on purpose." Her voice rose with anger as she went on. "Hector stopped and called out to them. He said, 'Excuse me.'"

"The white boys stopped and turned. I got scared. They were looking for trouble. I could tell from their eyes. I pulled on Hector's arm. 'Come on. Forget it.' But one of the boys. He came back and got up in Hector's face. He said, 'You got a problem, spic?'"

"I said to Ramon. 'Do something.'" As she spoke, reliving the incident, Rosie choked up. She shook her head, putting her face in her hands. "I shouldn't have said that. It's all my fault."

"No, no, Rosalina. Do not say this. Ramon was a brave boy. He would protect my Hector, no matter what. You know that." Mrs. Navarro put an arm around Rosie's shoulders and pulled her into an embrace.

"Wait," I said, staring at these two women. The girlfriend of the deceased and the mother of the accused were hugging. "I'm missing something here."

Rosie picked her head up from Mrs. Navarro's fleshy shoulder. "Ramon stepped in between Hector and the boy. He told the boy to back off.

"'Or what?' the boy said, and Ramon hit him. The boy fell into his friends' arms. His friends laughed and shoved him at

Ramon, calling their friend names for getting hit by a smelly beaner."

"You're saying one of these boys who fought with Ramon beat him up?"

Rosie shook her head. "Not one. Two." Tears fell as Rosie continued, her sobbing making it difficult for her to speak clearly. "They knocked Ramon to the ground. I saw blood on the sidewalk where he hit his head. The two of them jumped on top of him and started punching him. They kept punching him, kicking him. I tried to pull them off, but they pushed me away." With pleading eyes, she stared at Mrs. Navarro. "I tried to stop them."

Mrs. Navarro nodded. "I know. I know."

"What about Hector? What was he doing while all this was going on?"

"He fought with the other one. The one that was really big. He was really strong. Hector couldn't beat him."

That explained the cuts and bruises Hector had when the police picked him up. The mug shot in the file revealed a badly beaten boy, his left eye swollen shut. He had several lacerations and a dark, puffy face the color of raw hamburger meat. The officers at the scene assumed the cuts, the scrapes and bruises were from Ramon defending himself.

Rosie wiped away her tears with trembling fingers, pressing her lips together in a tight line to stop her crying. She only moderately succeeded. Mrs. Navarro squeezed her arm tighter around the girl's shoulders, pulling her closer.

"I'm not getting something," I admitted. "If these boys did this, why did you tell the police it was Hector?"

"I was told to," Rosie said, her glistening eyes filling with more tears. "I had no choice."

I blinked. "Told to? By whom?"

She looked at me and swallowed hard. With encouragement from Mrs. Navarro, she opened her mouth to speak, then snapped it shut. Her whole body suddenly went stiff. Her puffy eyes widened. Something over my shoulder, out on the street behind us, had caught her attention. Spooked her.

"No," she said, suddenly adamant. "I have nothing to say to you. Go away. Both of you." She spun, yanked the screen door open, and ran inside. The door banged shut behind her. Rosie fumbled with the hook-and-eye lock until she got the screen door secure. Then she yelled at us again, much louder than was necessary. "Go away. Both of you. I won't talk to you. Ever."

She slammed the heavy interior door, and then I heard a deadbolt engage and the muffled rattle of a chain lock.

Something had scared the hell out of her. I looked at Mrs. Navarro for insight and found her staring out past the parking lot of old cars, past the fenced-in garbage bins, out to the street beyond. I followed her gaze and saw what had scared Rosie so badly.

A police patrol car. It cruised along slowly with two officers inside. They stared up at us out of impossibly dark sunglasses as they passed. There was something not right about that cruiser. I just couldn't place it.

SHERIFF'S DEPUTY SUZIE Jensen was late.

Sitting in my vintage, black '78 Firebird, parked at the far end of the Kroger's parking lot, I had the tee-top open and my sunglasses on. The early afternoon sun baked the air with a hot, dry intensity, making me almost wish for winter. I checked the time on my cell phone for the zillionth time and thought again about running into the supermarket to grab a cold bottle of water while I waited.

About to do just that, I climbed out of my car, shut the door, and key-fobbed the after-market alarm system I'd had installed in my mint-condition, painstakingly restored, black beauty (did I say how much I love my car) only to have my quick trek to the store interrupted by the short burp of a police siren. I shaded my eyes to see a sheriff's cruiser shooting diagonally across the lot at me, followed closely by an unmarked, dark blue Crown Victoria.

"Perfect timing," I groused sarcastically under my breath while I needlessly waved. Suzie pulled up beside my ride and got out, squashing a Smokey-the-Bear hat down over her spiky, punk-rock blond hair. The unmarked car pulled in beside her. I watched as a heavy-set Latino got out. He wore a cheap blazer and dark slacks, a blue dress shirt with the collar pulled open, and his thin, black tie yanked down.

"Hell, if I wanted heat like this, I'd live in Miami." He stuck out a meaty right hand. His dark eyes sparkled with mirth and compassion. "Detective Francis Ferlito. My friends call me Frank."

I shook his hand, immediately liking him. "Frank. I'm Grace deHaviland."

"The bounty hunter, I know." He smiled. Meant to charm, and it did. "Suzie told me a little about what you're working on."

"What little she gave me, Frank," Suzie said, playfully scolding me.

After leaving Mrs. Navarro's place in Whitehall, I'd called my best friend, Suzie, a county sheriff's deputy with over eleven years on the job, asking if she knew anyone on the Reynoldsburg police force she could trust. She said she knew a guy over there, a detective with twenty-plus years in, and offered to set up a meeting.

And here we were.

"It's not my case," Ferlito said, handing me a file folder. "But this is what you asked for. Care to fill me in?"

"And me," Suzie added with an impish grin.

I flipped open the file with Suzie looking over my shoulder. In it were statements from the three witnesses Rosie told me about, the ones conspicuously missing from my reports: OSU students Jason Dunn, Teddy Daggs, and Dick Hansen. Inside the file, not included with the bail papers I'd received, were supplemental-to-arrest reports written by the arresting officers; Sgt. Troy Stevenson and Officer David McNamara.

As I read, I asked Ferlito questions. "Have you read this?"

"I glanced at them on the way over here. What's catching your eye?"

"The statements from the three witnesses. They're strikingly—"

"Similar," Suzie finished for me, looking up. "Almost word for word."

"Coached," I concluded.

Ferlito gave a shrug, a little defensively. "Three kids saw the same thing. So what?"

I flipped the file closed.

"I just came from talking with Rosalina Lopez. She told me Hector Navarro didn't beat up Ramon Ruiz. According to her, it was these three college boys."

Ferlito shook his head. "Not according to her statement. I read enough to know she fingered the Navarro boy."

He was regurgitating the company line, so I switched gears. "What can you tell me about these two cops? Stevenson and McNamara?"

He leaned back on the fender of his unmarked car, the engine clicking as it cooled, and folded his arms over his chest. Suspicion clouded his face. "Troy Stevenson is a veteran cop with almost as much time in as me. McNamara?" He shrugged. "He's a newbie. Got a few years in. Decent guy, though."

He'd elaborated about McNamara but not Troy Stevenson. *Interesting.* It was only a thread, but I pulled on it. "What is it about Stevenson you don't like?"

Frank Ferlito looked away, then grunted before giving me a sly smile, no doubt appreciating my lightning-quick ability to pick up on his nuances. "Okay. My opinion. He's a muscle-head, redneck racist. Abuses his authority and is quick to mete out his own brand of justice. He squeaked out of a questionable shooting a few years back. Has had more than his share of excessive force complaints. In short? He's a dirtbag with a badge."

"But not McNamara?"

He dropped his hands to the hood of the car and shook his head. "Naw. Dave's a good kid. Too much of a follower, maybe, but he'll grow out of that with experience."

I nodded, thinking about what Rosie had told me, what Mrs. Navarro and I spoke about after Rosie had gone inside and the police cruiser had moved on. That still bothered me. But it wasn't until later that I realized why.

Ferlito interrupted my musings. "Okay, I gave up what I know. Now it's your turn. Why's a bounty hunter so interested in the two arresting officers instead of your runner?"

"I told you. Rosie Lopez gave me a different version of what happened that night." He nodded, and I told him and Suzie what she'd said—about the fight and the three boys beating up Hector and Ramon. How she was told to lie about it. To say Hector did it.

Ferlito came off the car fender and began to pace. "Told by whom? You know what you're suggesting, right?"

I nodded. And not any happier about it than he was.

He looked straight at me. "How could anyone make her do that?"

"Because she had no choice."

"No choice?" Suzie asked. "Why not?"

"Because she's an illegal." I'd learned this from Mrs. Navarro. After Rosie slammed her door in our faces. "Her whole family is. She was told if she didn't say Hector did this, she and her whole family would be deported."

I explained to Ferlito and Suzie about the police car cruising past Rosie's apartment and what had bothered me about that. Many municipal police cars in and around the county are white, but each municipality has its own color stripes and gold shields painted on the sides of their patrol cars. The shield on the door of this cruiser wasn't a replica of the Whitehall police badge, the town where Rosie lived.

The emblem on the side of this patrol car read: POLICE. REYNOLDSBURG.

Ferlito shook his head. "That doesn't make sense."

On that, I had to agree with him. What reason would two cops from Reynoldsburg have for cruising around Rosie Lopez's neighborhood, way outside their jurisdiction? Maybe they'd taken it on themselves to look for Hector Navarro? Maybe not. We wouldn't know by speculating. We'd only get the truth when we talked to Hector. Or someone spoke to the two cops. Ferlito maybe?

I was about to suggest that when the radio in Frank Ferlito's Crown Vic crackled with a call. Between bursts of static, I caught: *"...armed assault...shots fired...units responding... Sun Valley Court..."*

"Sun Valley Court," I said. "There's something about that...."

"It's a cul-de-sac by the golf course," Ferlito offered. "In Reynoldsburg."

"No, no," I said. Then it hit me. I flipped open the file I was still holding. I pointed to one of the witness statements. "Here it is. Jason Dunn lives on Sun Valley Court."

"Shit!" Ferlito shouted, already running to his car. "The unit responding, that's Stevenson and McNamara."

"I'll drive," Suzie said to me. "Get in."

Lights and sirens on and tires squealing, Ferlito spun his Crown Vic around and shot for the parking lot exit. Suzie was right behind, with me holding on for dear life. It was a ten-mile drive, which we made in four minutes.

Sun Valley Court was in a solid, upper-middle-class development of quarter-acre properties with cookie-cutter, single-family, two-story homes on neatly maintained lawns littered with bicycles and skateboards, basketball hoops, jump ropes, and baseball mitts. A Reynoldsburg cruiser sat at the curb one house in from the intersection.

Frank Ferlito slammed to an angled stop in front of the cruiser. Suzie slid in behind him and jumped out. "This is a police matter," she yelled to me. "Stay in the car."

"Like hell," I yelled back.

Suzie circled around the police cars, using them as cover, two hands holding her service Glock out in front. She came up behind Ferlito, who I was surprised to see holding a .38 revolver. I didn't think anyone carried wheel guns anymore.

"Sergeant Stevenson," he called out. "What'd'ya got?"

A bulked-out cop in a uniform two sizes too small for him— to show off his bulging biceps and Arnold Schwarzenegger-like pecs—peered over his shoulder, his service weapon held in a classic Weaver-stance. "We've got it, detective. Thanks."

A few feet to Stevenson's left stood a rail-thin, young blonde cop. His stance was less rock-steady as he gulped air and ping-ponged his eyes from Stevenson to Ferlito, then to the two young men standing in the front yard.

The frightening-looking white kid with the gun to his head had to be Jason Dunn because the guy holding the gun, with his dark, shaved head and scraggly goatee, I knew was Hector

Navarro from his mug shot photo. He also had an arm around Dunn's throat in a choke-hold.

I circled around to the right, crouching but without drawing my weapon. More than enough guns were on the scene already.

I called out. "What's going on, Hector?"

He swung his attention toward me, stepping back and pulling Dunn along with him. Dunn winced, the gun barrel grinding into his temple. "Don't come any closer. Who are you?"

"I'm here to help, Hector. Tell us what's going on?"

"This *asesino!*" He shook Dunn. "He killed my friend. He killed Ramon."

"I know." My confirmation shocked him.

And everyone else.

Ferlito snapped his head in my direction, as did the two uniform cops. Troy Stevenson narrowed his eyes into an *if-looks-could-kill* stare. "You don't know what you're talking about. Who is this bitch?"

The question was fired at Ferlito. He responded. "Shut up, Troy."

"That's not true, Hector," McNamara said. "We have witnesses. Statements that say you beat up Ramon."

Hector swung his gun at McNamara. "Lies! They all lied!"

Everyone tensed: The cops crouching drew a tighter bead on Hector. Dunn screamed like a baby. Suzie and I exchanged glances.

I shouted, "Don't do that, Hector! Please. We don't want anyone getting hurt. Look, I'm not armed." I held both my hands out. Empty. "See? Let's just talk. I spoke with Rosie. She told me what really happened."

Sergeant Stevenson took an angry step forward. "We know what happened. Let's put an end to this."

"Stand down, Troy," Ferlito commanded. "Now!"

"Yes. We do know what happened, Sergeant." I took a step in. "We know you and your partner coerced a young girl into lying. You told her if she didn't, you'd have her and her whole family deported. We know you made sure she didn't recant her story by driving around her neighborhood. Intimidating her. The only thing we don't know is why?"

"That's ridiculous. Are you going to listen to this, Frank?"

"Yes, I am," Ferlito said. "Now, for the last time, Troy. Put your gun away."

"Oh. I see how it is." He glared at Ferlito, then at me. "All you wetbacks sticking together? Is that it?"

"Shut up, Troy," Ferlito said through clenched teeth.

Suzie used the distraction to make her way over to Hector. "Give me the gun, Hector." She held out a hand. "We know what happened. We'll take care of this."

Still afraid, he backed up. "No! This *asesino* killed Ramon. He and his friends. They killed him, and you need to know it."

"They will," I said.

Suzie nodded. "I promise. You have my word."

A minute ticked by. Then another. I felt as if my heart had stopped beating and my lungs had stopped taking in air as we waited, and I hoped, prayed, Hector would do the right thing.

He did.

He relaxed his grip around Jason Dunn's throat and handed his gun to Suzie.

Taking it, Suzie holstered her own weapon, spun Dunn around and snapped handcuffs around his wrists. "Jason Dunn, you're under arrest for the murder of Ramon Ruiz."

"What! This is crazy," Sgt. Stevenson blurted out. He drew a bead on Hector. "He's a dangerous criminal. Stop him before he gets away."

It took me less than a nanosecond to realize his intentions. He was going to shoot Hector down. Shut him up by killing him. Say he was trying to escape.

"No!" I shouted, drawing my .45 fast.

Frank Ferlito was even faster. He put his .38 to Stevenson's head. "Drop it, or I'll blow your racist head off."

Troy Stevenson dropped his gun. He turned to McNamara. "Dave. Do something."

David McNamara did. He holstered his service gun and said, "Shut up, Sarge. It's all over."

Suzie led Dunn to where the other cops stood. Told him to keep still while she secured McNamara with his own handcuffs. Ferlito did the same with Troy Stevenson. Over the ratcheting of cuffs, Ferlito said, "You're both under arrest for entering a false police report, for intimidation, for witness tampering, and conspiracy to cover up a murder." He added, "For starters."

I checked on Hector to see if he was okay. He was, so I joined the others. I grabbed Stevenson by his bulging arm and made him face me. "Why? Just tell me why?"

His smile was cold. And cruel. "I've got nothing to say until I speak to my lawyer. And my union rep."

I would get no answers from him. Maybe we would never know exactly why they'd done it.

"Come on," Suzie said to Jason Dunn, moving him toward her sheriff's car.

And it was from that scared young man I got my answer.

"What's going to happen now?" he asked, but not to Suzie or Frank Ferlito or even me. His question was directed at Sergeant Troy Stevenson. "What's going to happen now, Uncle Troy?"

###

BLING, BLING

MIGHTY MO' MAC was not his real name. It was Myron Epps. He wasn't born or raised in South Central LA. Not even in the South Bronx. He grew up in Granville, Ohio, a small, rural college town thirty-five miles northeast of Columbus. No, his mom wasn't a crack whore selling herself out of a double-wide. She was a professor of English at Dennison University. And no, his dad wasn't serving five-fifteen in prison. He served on the Granville Board of Trustees.

But being a young man growing up in a well-to-do family in Middle America did not sell rap albums. And ever since before he could remember, all Myron Epps ever wanted to do was be a rap star. And not just any rap star. Myron wanted to be the biggest, the baddest rap star there ever was.

Rap stars grew up in LA and New York, even Detroit. Not places like Granville, Ohio. They had names like Tupac and Snoop Dogg and 50 Cent. Not Myron Epps. Most of all, they had street cred. They had reps. They had juice.

Mo' Mac had credibility; he had a reputation. He had the juice. So what if it was all a lie. "Who's this?" he asked.

I offered him my business card. It read simply:

Grace deHaviland
Bail Enforcement Specialist

129

Mo' turned from the wall of windows where he stood, staring out at an Olympic-size pool surrounded by a landscaped patio with rock outcroppings and flowing waterfalls and tropical plantings with flowers and a wave slide and tiki torches and strung with lantern lights and a wet bar and a smoking B-B-Q pit, all overlooking the forested banks of the Scioto River below. Good-looking people in barely there bathing suits frolicked and drank and ate, all to the booming beat of rap music with bass so heavy it vibrated the glass and the whole house. It sounded like N.W.A. or maybe Public Enemy, but what did I know? Rap's not my thing.

A short, rotund figure, Mo' Mac took the card with pudgy fingers full of gold. He wore an open silk shirt with the sleeves rolled two turns up his arms. Sweat rings darkened his armpits, and he had enough gold draped around his neck to make King Midas jealous. Oh, and diamond studs the size of nickels in each ear.

He scrutinized the card with a furrowed brow. I wondered if maybe he couldn't read. Finally, he looked at the man standing beside me. His attorney, Saul Rosenfeld. Rosenfeld answered the door when I rang. He'd led me into the vast living space in the rapper's palatial mansion nestled on the banks of the Scioto River, north of Columbus.

"Bail Enforcement. What's that?"

I told him, "Bounty hunter."

He arched a thick black eyebrow. "Really?"

I nodded. "Really."

The eyebrow still raised, he said to Rosenfeld, "She's the one's gonna get Jimmy?"

An older, conservative fellow, Saul Rosenfeld wore a dark blue suit with a white shirt and red tie. A man with a thin build and darkly tanned features, he had a full head of white hair and sparkling white teeth. He shrugged. "I guess."

Mo grinned. "No shit?"

"No shit," I said. "I'd like to ask you a few questions. Get some background information on Jimmy Dolens."

"A sweet sista like you, darling. Ax me anything."

Being half-Latina, I have dusky brown skin, long, wavy black hair, and my eyes are emerald green like my mom's, so I get that sista stuff a lot. I didn't bother to correct him.

Mo' hooked an arm out, aiming to drape it over my shoulder.

I sidestepped out from under, smiling politely.

He frowned, not amused.

But his wife was. LaKendra sat on one of two facing couches by the fireplace. She flipped noisily through a copy of Variety magazine draped on her lap, snapping her gum. She snickered. Big, gold hoop earrings dangled from her ears. She wore silver, glittery short-shorts and a white sleeveless shirt she had tied between her ample boobs to reveal her bare, brown belly and the diamond stud in her navel that exactly matched the one in her nose.

LaKendra had a music career of her own before teaming up with Mo' Mac a few years back. A duet that led to a tumultuous marriage: think Whitney and Bobby on that one. By all accounts, neither the marriage nor the partnership had done anything to stop the tail-spin their careers were in. Not unlike the rest of hip-hop and the music business in general.

"You better watch yourself, Mo'," LaKendra said, nodding at me. "This cat's got claws, baby. And a bite too. Am I right, honey?"

"Ain't you got something to do?" Mo' asked. "Paint your nails or something equally as important?"

"Better than watching you make a fool of your own damn self?" She snapped her fingers and shook her head. Her gold hoops caught the light, winking. "I don't think so."

Mo' raised his arms, then slapped them down to his side, gazing around the gargantuan living room as if looking for help. He settled on Rosenfeld. "Saul. Do something with her, would ya?"

They were like squabbling siblings.

Rosenfeld tried to not look put upon. He failed. "Kendra, perhaps now would be a good time to look at those contracts the studio sent over. I have them in the kitchen."

LaKendra slapped her magazine down. "Fine. Whatever."

Rosenfeld put a hand to the small of her back, hovering just above her glittery spandex-encased bubble-butt, and guided her out of the room.

"We don't pay you enough for what you put up with, Saul," LaKendra said. "You know that?"

Rosenfeld sighed. "I know it."

If Mo' heard the exchange or cared, he didn't show it. He led me toward the front foyer. The ceilings throughout the house were twelve feet high, the walls painted a creamy white with expensive-looking blonde wood trim and bleached wood floors. The foyer was laid with tile so white I thought about putting my sunglasses back on. We started down a hallway. Memory lane. The walls were covered with framed CD covers and professionally shot photographs of Mo' and LaKendra on tour in various concert venues. The covers and the photos were individually lit with their own spotlight.

"What'd'ya wanna know about Jimmy? That he's a thieving, slimy, back-stabbin' dawg. That he ripped me off for over forty-million bucks. That he left me high and dry with egg turd on my face. That if I ever got my hands on him, I'd choke him 'til his eyes popped and his sockets bled. That's what I know about Jimmy Dawg Dolens."

Colorful.

What I knew about Jimmy Dolens was he was a financial management guru by trade, specializing in the entertainment industry. That he spent the last seven years as Mo' Mac's business manager until Mo fired him for, among other things, negligence, breach of conduct, misdirecting funds, and dereliction of fiduciary responsibility.

I also knew that the state's attorney general's office had him arrested six months ago, charging him with fraud, theft of services, and grand larceny.

Now out on bail and countersuing Mo' Mac for hundreds of thousands of dollars, his criminal trial was scheduled to start next week. The day before yesterday, Jimmy Dolens missed a pre-trial court appearance. That caused the judge to issue a bench warrant. The ink on the warrant wasn't dry before Dolens' bail bondman—on the hook for a hundred thousand dollars—called me to "track his worthless ass down."

"That's all well and good," I said in response to Mo's rant. "But I'm more interested in where he might've gone. Who he might contact? Who might help him now that he's on the run?"

"Man, I wish he'd come to me." He slapped a fist into his palm. "I'd help his ass all right."

I was getting nowhere with, and a little tired of, Mo's pseudo-gangsta act. I grabbed the crock of his arm, pulling him to a stop. "Look. You want Dolens to get what he deserves. I get that."

"You do, do you? Tell me. What'd'ya think he deserves, huh? Prison? Jail time? That's for pussies, girl. Justice ain't no prison cell. For me, justice is you cap his ass."

"Really? For stealing money, he deserves to die?"

Mo' took a moment to think on that. Once he did, he shook his head, like something he ate didn't agree with him. "Grace? It's Grace, right? You any idea how many cribs I got?"

I shrugged. "A few."

He liked that. "Yeah, a few. I got me seven right here in the U.S. of A. This one and two more here in Ohio. I gots a castle in Scotland. Cost me twenty-seven million bucks to renovate it. I don't even know how much to buy it. I've stayed there twice. You wanna talk about cars?"

I didn't.

He waved a hand in the air. Every finger had a ring on it, all of them sparkling gold and silver and diamonds. "More 'an I can count. Bentleys, Mercedes, Ferraris, a Maserati. Cars I ain't even driven yet. I even owns an island somewhere down in the Caribbean. A whole island. All mine, you dig?"

I started to say I didn't give a—

But he wagged a finger in front of me.

"That ain't all. I gots planes and boats and them Jet Ski things, and I gots me a record collection that's sick. Old stuff on vinyl, on tape. CDs. Thousands of 'em. Hundreds of thousands of 'em. And you know what?"

Bored, I was forced to shake my head.

"Two of my cribs? They in foreclosure. The feds? They say I ain't paid taxes in over two years. Six million dollars I owe them. Plus interest and penalties. Dolens was supposed to do that for me. I got liens on my properties. I got liens on my assets. I got liens up my mutherfucking ass. All 'cause of Jimmy fuckin' Dolens."

"Then tell me where to find him."

Mo' looked around the hallway, frustrated. Like I hadn't been listening to him. He shrugged. "How the hell I know where he's at? He ain't talking to me. Ain't talking to none of my people, you know?" He looked around some more. "Ain't nobody out there gonna help him. He's burned all his friends. Ain't got no family. No bruthers, no sistas. His ex-wife, maybe. Mindy. You talk to her yet?"

"I went to her house before coming here. No answer. Left messages on her cell."

"Yeah. Well, anyone knows where Jimmy's at? It'll be Mindy."

From behind us, Saul Rosenfeld said, "I have an idea that might help."

In tandem, Mo' and I turned. I wondered how long he'd been standing there, listening. "Jimmy kept a small office downtown, leased by Mo's and Kendra's corporation. I have the keys. Could something there help you? I can take you if you'd like."

"That would be great."

Rosenfeld stepped to one side and waved us toward the front foyer. He looked at Mo'. "Kendra's in the kitchen. You two need to talk."

"Right." Mo' stuffed his hands in his pants pockets and walked away from us. His head bowed like the weight of a world was on his shoulders. I guessed it was. His financial world. He stopped at the foyer and turned back.

"Grace, you don't like me much." At my protest, he held up a hand. "It's cool. You don't get to where I'm at without reading people. And fast. Now I know, you're looking at me and saying to yourself, I ain't got no sympathy for ole Mo' Mac. He ain't raking in forty million a year like he used to but so what? He's for-closed on two cribs, but he's got five more he can live in. He can maybe sell off a few of them, too, or that castle of his in Scotland or his Caribbean Island to settle up with the IRS deal. His shit ain't so bad. Not like he'll be on no unemployment line any time soon. You be thinking that, and you'd be right."

He swallowed hard. "But it ain't all about the bling."

"What's it about, Mo'?"

"It's about the work. It's about drive, pouring your heart all in your art. It's about what I do and how I do it. It's about delivering product to the people. It's about me being me. The whole package. It's about—"

"Your rep."

He smiled. I was getting it. Getting him. "That's right, girl. It's about the rep. I ain't like other people. Never have been, never will. I do what I do 'cause I love it and people respect me 'cause of it. The bling? That's just icing on the side. But to do what I do? People's got to respect me. That's what Jimmy Dolens took from me. That's what he stole. You dig?"

I nodded. And maybe I did, a little.

"Good. So do me a solid."

Skeptical, I said, "Ask, but no promises."

"Fair enough. What I'm axing is this. When you bag Jimmy D's, you call me."

"Why?"

"I wanna see him going down. I need that. You feel me?"

I nodded. "I feel you. But no promises."

Jimmy Dolens downtown office was on Gay Street, next to the old Modern Finance Building. It had two large windows and an alcove for an administrative assistant. I sat at the big oak desk while Saul Rosenfeld sat in one of two director chairs, watching me. He looked grateful to be able to sit and just relax. I let him.

Several metal filing cabinets lined one wall, there was a small coffee table, and two low, overstuffed chairs set off in the corner. The walls were filled with dozens of pictures of Jimmy with rap stars (Snoop Dogg, Lil Wayne, 8Ball, Eminem); Jimmy with movie people (Denzel Washington, Danny Glover, Spike Lee, Russell Crowe); and Jimmy with rappers-turned-movie people (Ice Cube, Mark Wahlberg, Ludacris, Will Smith).

"What are you hoping to find?"

Tossing the desk drawers, I said, "Hard to say. Client lists. Contact information of people he knows. Places he's known to frequent."

There was no computer in the office. It had probably been seized by the authorities when they arrested Dolens. There was no BlackBerry, no Rolodex. Even his files had been picked through and cleaned out. The trip to the office was beginning to look like a waste of time.

Because Rosenfeld sat there, staring, I felt obligated to say something, to talk. "Most people are creatures of habit. They have a comfort zone. They do the same things, eat at the same restaurants, go to the same movie theater, buy their cigarettes at the same corner market, their lattes at the same Starbucks. Change makes people jittery. They avoid it, and that makes my job easier."

I closed the last drawer in the desk. It, and the office, was a bust.

"Tell me more about Mo' and LaKendra."

"What's to tell?" he said. "Mo' and Kendra are into the IRS for millions in unpaid back taxes. When they started calling, Jimmy's…shortcomings surfaced. They've foreclosed on properties that are underwater. Unsellable. They've defaulted on dozens of loans. Their credit's been stretched to the limit, with Jimmy taking out loans to cover old loans. It's a mess."

He shook his head like a disappointed father. "They're blaming it all on Jimmy, of course. Accusing him of stealing millions over the years while keeping them in the dark about risky business investments he's entered into, using their names to get in, exaggerating the value of their assets to get credit, defaulting on payments even after they've been extended. And, of course, finally, not paying their taxes."

"And did he?" I asked. "Do all those things?"

Rosenfeld shrugged and looked at the carpet. "It's like a messy divorce. There's blame enough to go around. Jimmy took advantage and did things he shouldn't have, hid things from them he shouldn't have. When the gravy train started to sputter, he scrambled to stay ahead. As is inevitable in these cases, he couldn't."

Sensing his reluctance to go on, I prodded. "But there's more."

"Mo' and Kendra didn't do anything to help their situation. They kept buying cars and houses and planes and jewelry and clothes. You want to talk about vacations and parties? Would make you sick the money they spend. Mo' and Kendra kept acting like nothing was wrong. Like Jimmy didn't tell them a thing." He sat up and sighed. "That's a crock, too. He warned them. I warned them. We haven't had a new record contract in over three years. With nothing new in the pipeline, sales tanked. The tours weren't selling out. Then they weren't even getting booked. Anyone could see the income stream was drying up. All they had to do was look."

He sat back heavily. "They figured something would come up. It did. The houselights. Now, the bill is due." He looked past me out the window, to the street below, and maybe even further than that. "You ask me? Sure, Jimmy's a thief, but Mo' and Kendra were as complacent as if they were co-conspirators."

I got up, stretched, and wandered to the window to contemplate my next move. I looked to the street below. Middle of the day, traffic was light. Across the street, the outdoor tables at Café Brioso were filling up with the early lunch time crowd. Just another day.

I watched for a few minutes, then turned away. "You just said they hadn't had a new recording contract in years, but back at the house, you took Kendra into the kitchen to discuss new contracts the studio sent over. What was that all about?"

Rosenfeld shifted in his seat, suddenly antsy, his lips pressed into a thin line. Stalling, he got up. He buttoned his jacket, tugging at the cuff-linked, powder blue sleeves underneath. I wondered how hard Mo' and Kendra's recession was hitting him. Then I saw the Rolex watch. Maybe not so hard. He cleared his throat.

"Arco Records has made an offer. A deal for a new album. And tour dates."

Good news, I would've thought, but Rosenfeld looked like he'd just swallowed a guppy. I asked the natural but apparently stupid question. "That's good, isn't it?"

"Normally, sure." He cleared his throat. "Here's the thing, and you can't repeat this to anyone. There is a deal on the table. A lucrative one. But there's a catch."

And I guessed what it was. "They don't want Mo'."

He nodded. "It's Kendra and only Kendra. She's got to cut Mo' out, or there's no deal."

"She going to do it?"

He shrugged again. "Has to. No choice."

"Mo' know yet?"

Rosenfeld consulted his watch. The Rolex. "Probably by now. I reviewed the financials with Kendra while you were talking with Mo'. The two of them are incorporated. Partners. Fifty-fifty. She's got to get Mo' to relinquish any involvement or no deal."

I whistled. "That'll be hard to take." I thought about street cred and reps. About juice. "How's he going to react?"

"In a word? Badly. With all this, I'm afraid it'll crush him."

"You have some nerve!" The voice came from a petit blonde woman who appeared at the office door. "What are you doing here, Saul Rosenfeld?"

Rosenfeld spun. "Mindy?"

Mindy must be Mindy Dolens. Jimmy's ex. Dressed in a cream-colored trench coat, cinched tight around her impossibly thin, stick-figure waist, she had mousy blonde hair and pinched features. She carried a large black bag trapped between her arm and side, the straps high on her shoulder.

DAVID DELEE

"You have no right to be here. This is Jimmy's private office."

Rosenfeld took a step toward her. "Mindy…"

"You have no right, Saul." Her eyes brimmed with tears. Fighting them back, she pushed an errant lock of hair off her face. "Why? Why are you here?"

"We're looking for Jimmy," I offered. "We could use your help."

Her eyes flicked to me, murderous in their anger, wide in their shock at my audacity. "You can't be serious?" She turned her attention back to Rosenfeld. "I won't help you hurt Jimmy, Saul. How could you? You were his friend."

He seemed to melt a full suit size under her stare. "Mindy, I…"

"You are unbelievable."

She spun and bolted down the hall.

I ran to the door and called out, "Mrs. Dolens. Please."

She was already at the stairwell and pounding down the steps. To Rosenfeld, I said, "Stay here."

"Where are you going?"

"To get Jimmy Dolens."

I raced to the top of the stair, then paused, waiting, listening to Mindy's heeled shoes banging down the steps below me. I counted to ten. I didn't want to stop her anymore. I'd decided instead to follow her.

The door downstairs opened. I slowed. It swung shut with a click. I picked up my pace, reaching the door—an old glass and wood frame thing—and stood off to one side, glanced out, first to the right, then the left. I spotted Mindy walking at a brisk pace, crossing the street, already half a block away.

I stepped outside, keeping to the left side of the sidewalk, staying close to the buildings. If Mindy glanced over, I could turn and pretend to window-shop. Unfortunately, the buildings were mostly vacant. Only a large auction banner in the window to catch anyone's attention. It would have to do.

But my luck held. Mindy dashed across High Street without a glance back. She continued west, a woman in a hurry. I jogged across the intersection against the light and cursed the horn-blowing idiot who tried to run me down, more worried it would catch Mindy's attention than for my own safety. My heart thumped as I speculated where she might lead me, hoping it would be to Jimmy Dolens.

Both pedestrian and vehicular traffic picked up on the other side of High Street. That worked to my advantage. Keeping Mindy in sight, I zigzagged through the crowd, closing in on her but using them to conceal my approach.

Settling behind two men in business suits, I shrugged off my *Just Cavalli* leather jacket. When I emerged from behind them, I had my jacket draped over my arm; my thick, black hair wound in a tight ponytail; and my cell phone trapped between my ear and shoulder, carrying on a one-sided conversation.

Mindy had come to Jimmy's office for a reason. What it was, I had no idea. I thought about calling Rosenfeld and asking him to look around to see what I'd missed, but I nixed that idea. If she led me to Jimmy, it wouldn't matter.

Tired of talking to myself, I snapped the phone shut in time to see Mindy making her way to the next intersection. Wall Street. Unlike the one in New York, this Wall Street was an alley at best, and the only transactions taking place here happened after dark and involved drugs or sex.

At the corner, she glanced back.

I turned my back to her, dropping two quarters into the nearest parking meter for cover. I waited a heartbeat, then glanced over my shoulder. She was gone. I jogged the half block to Wall Street, stopped at the corner of the Diamond Exchange building, and peeked down the alley.

Mindy was the only person in sight. A block down, heading away from me.

I waited until she reached the end of the block, a three-story red brick building. Across the street, there was a single-story building with a large, open bay door. Cars were parked inside. I could hear tools clanging and the loud blast of an impact drill. Beyond it was Elm Street, then the parking lot Mindy appeared heading for.

I ran, threading my arms back into my jacket. There were probably a hundred cars parked in that lot. If she climbed into one of them before I got there, I'd lose her. I reached the end of the building and the parking lot beyond it. I stopped and poked my head around the corner, hoping to see her threading her way between cars, maybe getting into one. I didn't.

Damn it.

A sea of cars, gleaming hot in the noontime sun. Out of options, I entered the lot, feeling exposed, walking along the first row, stooping so I could look through rear windows, listening for the telltale sound of a car door opening or closing, an engine starting up.

I reached the end of the row. Nothing. Fearing I'd lost my best lead, anxiety soured my stomach. I told myself patience was the key and started down the next row. A dark blue SUV, a red Miata, a banged-up late model Civic. My heart tripping. If a car suddenly started up and shot out of the lot, I was powerless to stop it.

My car was three blocks away, still parked at the curb on Gay Street.

She'd be gone.

Walking. I stooped and looked. Walked on.

A gray Lexus. An old Mercury Sable station wagon. A red Volkswagen Beetle. There. In a late model, green Corolla pulled in grille first, sat two figures. I bent low using the VW bug for cover. Even with my dark sunglasses, I had to raise a hand to further block the intense sun. The passenger in the Corolla had straight, mousy, blonde hair.

Had to be Mindy.

And in the driver's seat: Jimmy Dolens!

I drew my weapon, a Kimber .45, and my badge case. With the .45 in my left hand, I held my shield visible in my right, my wrists locked, one over the other. I duckwalked behind the Corolla, low, came up along the driver's side, and tapped the glass with the heavy barrel of the .45. Dolens jumped like I'd zapped him with a Taser.

"Bail enforcement!" I yelled through the glass. "Step out of the car! Keep your hands where I can see them!"

He twisted some more, then reached for the door handle. The lock disengaged with a click; the door opened.

I tensed. "Slowly!"

From inside the car Dolens was yelling. "—led her right to me. Jesus Christ!"

Mindy protested weakly, "I didn't."

He banged the door into the car beside it. Jimmy Dolens rolled out between the narrow opening. Tall and lanky, he came up all arms and legs. His skin was dark as crude, a string bean of a guy in an oversized gray sweatshirt, jeans, and sneakers.

I took a step back. "Get your hands where I can see them. Raise 'em!"

"Yeah, yeah." Jimmy Dolens stood up to his six-foot-four-inch frame, his hands raised in the air, his eyes darting around, running through his options. He had none.

The passenger door slammed open, and Mindy jumped out. "Don't hurt him! Please!"

My eyes darted to Mindy, but I kept the .45 trained on Jimmy. "Stay where you are, and no one'll get hurt. Just stay calm and do exactly what I tell you." I tucked my badge into the back pocket of my jeans and waved Jimmy toward me.

"Put your hands behind your head, and face the car."

Jimmy did as he was told. I holstered the .45 and swung his arms behind his back, cuffing him with flexicuffs. Mindy watched us over the roof of the Corolla, worry in her eyes. I turned Jimmy around. In his eyes, I saw a strange mixture of anger and resignation.

"Is there anything I can offer you?"

I shook my head.

He slumped against the car trunk, resignation beating out anger. "Didn't think so." Mindy rushed over to be with him, stroking his arm and muttering, "I'm sorry." Watching them, I made two phone calls.

The first was to Suzie Jensen, a deputy sheriff, and my best friend. We'd joined the sheriff's department together ten years earlier, just a few years out of high school. She was still with them, a road supervisor now. I hadn't lasted two years.

When she answered, I told her what I had and asked if she'd provide transport to Police Division Headquarters. She agreed. Of course, she agreed. She's my friend. Besides, she'd get credit as the arresting officer, help beef up her stats.

While we waited, I made my second call, this one to Saul Rosenfeld. I told him I had Jimmy in custody and would bring him to Division shortly.

"That's great. Great news. What happens now?"

I told him. Once we got Jimmy to headquarters, we'd take him in and let the desk sergeant know what we had. At that point, Suzie—as the arresting officer—would escort Jimmy through the booking process. Photos, prints, the whole works. Then he'd be put in a cell and wait to be arraigned. He'd be re-charged. If the D.A. wanted to play hardball, additional charges could be tacked on.

What I didn't tell Rosenfeld was while all that was going on, I'd be on the phone with Jimmy's bail bondsman, making arrangements to have the bounty payment deposited into my bank account. This gig meant ten thousand dollars to my positive cash flow.

"What about Mindy?" he asked, interrupting my thoughts.

She could be charged with aiding and abetting, conspiracy, harboring a fugitive. That would be up to the D.A. But I told her and Jimmy that if they stayed cool, I'd forget to report her involvement.

"Good, good," Rosenfeld said approvingly. "Kendra called. She told Mo' 'bout the studio's offer."

With a held breath, I asked, "And...?"

"Like I expected, he blew up. A lot of screaming and shouting, throwing things. Making threats."

"What kind of threats?"

Rosenfeld poo-pooed it. "Words. A lot of yelling. Nothing more. Mo's all bluster, no bite."

"You sure?"

"Yeah. I've known Mo' a long time. All talk."

"And Kendra? She's okay?"

"She will be, but boy, did she go for broke. She cut Mo' out completely. Told him the partnership, the marriage, all of it was over. A clean break."

I winced. "That hurts."

"I guess. Wasn't much of a marriage to speak with."

"Still," I said, "have his wife send him packing while she goes on to do a new album, leaving him teetering on the edge of bankruptcy. Where's the street cred in that?"

"Yeah. Well, you've got Jimmy for him. That's something. He could use some good news today. I'll call him and let him know."

"No!" Damn it.

Rosenfeld hung up before I could tell him that was a really bad idea.

Deputy Suzie Jensen drove us up Ludlow Street to the back entrance of Division Headquarters. She pulled her cruiser into the curb across the street. I sat in the back with Jimmy; Mindy followed close behind in the Corolla. Once we parked, Suzie flipped the emergency lights on, got out, and opened the back door, all the while scanning the street for problems neither of us expected. Old habits.

I climbed out and did the same, then leaned over and urged Jimmy out. Cars lined one side of the street, and further down, there was a parking lot full of cars and people milling around. The police lights piqued their interest. A few stopped to watch, hoping to see something exciting.

"Let's get him processed." Suzie smiled, relaxed. "Then you can thank me with a drink at the Wooden Nickel. First round's on you."

I smiled back. "Goes without saying." To Jimmy, I said, "Watch your head."

I held a protective hand out. When he'd fully emerged from the backseat, I took hold of his arm. Suzie slammed the door shut and did the same on his opposite side.

"Ready?" Suzie asked.

I said, "Ready."

But we weren't.

We spun, hearing the sudden screech of tires from a car fishtailing around the corner, spewing thick white clouds of smoke behind it. It was a black Maybach, a $400,000 luxury car made in Germany. The car righted itself, then slammed on the brakes, sliding to a stop a dozen feet from where we stood, leaving Suzie and me feeling a bit flatfooted.

The driver's door flung open.

I can't say I was surprised seeing Mo' push his bulk up and out of the driver's seat. What did shock me was the Glock in his right hand.

Suzie shouted, "Gun!"

We both drew weapons while Suzie pushed Jimmy down to the ground.

I shouted, "Mindy! Get down!" Then I took a step toward Mo'. "You don't want to do this." I whispered to Suzie, "Stay with Jimmy; I can talk him down."

I stepped wide, circling away from Suzie and Jimmy, drawing Mo's attention to me. I held my .45 in a classic Weaver stance.

From my peripheral vision, I notice a couple of cops a dozen yards back moving quickly toward us from police headquarters while several people in the parking lot surged to the curb, eager to watch, to see something 'go down.'

"Mutherfucker stole from me. He needs to pay."

Mo' lined his pistol up on Jimmy, holding it sideways, gangsta-style.

"You don't want to do this, Mo'," I said.

"I can't let 'im get away with dissing me. I can't. He's gotta pay."

Suzie crouched over Jimmy, her 9mm in her hand, tracking Mo'.

"It's not going to be Jimmy who pays, Mo'. Not if you do this." I moved slowly, closing the gap between us.

"You don't know what you're talking 'bout. Man fucked my rep. Needs to be put down, like a dawg."

"You try putting him down," I nodded toward Suzie, "one of us is putting you down. We can't stop that, Mo'. Only you can. Now put the gun down."

He glanced over to the crowd gathering at the edge of the parking lot, watching us. It had swelled to a dozen people or more. I felt the presence of the cops moving up behind me. If I couldn't talk him down soon, this was going to end badly. Very badly.

From the crowd, someone yelled, "Hey, dat's Mo' Mac!" A young black man in cargo pants two sizes too big for him. "Can't let 'em get away with that, dawg!"

Jesus. My skin was prickly with sweat. "Don't listen to that shit, Mo'. Jimmy's going to pay for what he's done. I promise. He'll be going away for a long time."

"Jail? That don't mean jack shit."

Again, from the crowd: "Give it to 'im, Mo'!"

Suddenly another car wheeled around the corner. A black Beemer, coming on fast. The car stopped. Both front doors flung open. Saul Rosenfeld came out of the passenger side. LaKendra popped out of the driver's seat.

"Mo' Fuckin' Mac! What the hell you doing?"

Rosenfeld moved to the edge of the car door. "Kendra, don't."

But she'd already cleared her door and was marching toward Mo'. Her hands on her ample hips. Fisted. Her bitch full on.

I called out, "Kendra, stay back!"

She didn't listen.

Mo' had pivoted when the car first came around the corner. Now he turned. His gun aimed squarely at LaKendra. His pudgy face glistened with perspiration. His eyes were wide, jumping around. I wondered if he was on something.

LaKendra said, "Put that damn gun down, fool. You ain't shooting nobody. 'Cept your own damn self, you ain't careful."

Mo' took a step toward her. His brow hooded. His anger was palpable. And his arm rock steady holding the gun. "Who you think you is? Coming here, telling me what to do. You crazy, bitch. You gonna stop me from doing what's right?" He waved a hand at Jimmy. "After the shit you pulled today? You gonna go stepping out on me," —he slapped his chest with his hand— "then come here and tell me not to cap this low-life mutherfucker here?"

LaKendra's paced slowed. Something in her face told me she wasn't so sure about what Mo' would or wouldn't do. That maybe he had been pushed too far, pushed past his limit.

She held up her hands. Her voice became soft. "Mo', baby, listen, no…."

Behind me, I heard Suzie. She saw it, too. "Grace…"

I took off running. "Mo'! No! Don't!"

Mo' Mac turned the Glock straight up and down in his hand, now properly gripped to shoot. I shouted again, still running, close now. The two cops behind me were charging hard. I leaped.

He pulled the trigger. The recoil lifted Mo's hand.

The bullet struck LaKendra in the stomach. She staggered back, clutching at her gut. Blood leaked through her fingers. She looked up, wide-eyed.

I crashed into Mo'. His large puffy body fell forward. We hit the ground. The Glock flew out of his hand and skidded across the pavement. One of the cops dropped down beside us. He grabbed Mo's arms and pushed me away, flipping Mo' onto his stomach. He wrenched Mo's hands up and back, his knee grinding into Mo's back as he cuffed him. He wasn't gentle doing it.

I climbed to my feet as the cop hauled Mo' to his.

The other cop and Rosenfeld were on the ground beside LaKendra. The cop was shouting into his shoulder mic for a bus. Rosenfeld gripped her hand. She coughed. Blood bubbled up out of her mouth.

Suzie came up behind me and put a hand on my shoulder. "You okay?"

I glanced behind her, saw more cops had arrived. Two of them were walking Jimmy Dolens toward Division Headquarters, Mindy in tow, crying.

The cop with me held Mo' by the arm, firm. The ambulance sirens were already in the air, getting closer. The cop with LaKendra was doing CPR. There was nothing I could do.

Mo' had a confused look on his face. He was staring at his wife, watching her die. I stared at Mo'. "What were you thinking? Now you've lost everything."

At hearing my words, he turned to me. His expression shifted from confused to serene.

Then a smile spread across his face. "I didn't lose nuthin'. I fixed it." His smile grew wider. "I finally fixed it."

It was my turn to be confused. "Fixed it? How?"

Mo' didn't say. It was the crowd that gave me the answer. It had grown to twenty, maybe twenty-five people. Young people mostly. Blacks wearing their baseball caps sideways, their britches low, to expose their boxers. And Latinos in their wife-beater T-shirts and their plaid work shirts tied around their waists, a few Latinas, and a couple of young Asians.

"That was righteous, bro'."

"Yo, you rock, dude."

"Way to put that bitch down, man! That was whack."

"Mo' Mac! You the best."

"We loves you, Mo'."

I stepped back, shaking my head. But Mo', he was grinning.

"You hearing that? That's what I'm talking about." A second cop joined the first. They pulled him away from me, but Mo' kept shouting, "I gots it all going on now dawg! Who's da baddest nigga on the block now!" To me, he called out, "You watch. See how much my records be selling now, bitch!"

And the crowd cheered.

###

FINDING JESSIE

REBECCA GERRICK IGNORED the cell phone buzzing in her coat pocket. She couldn't take the call. Not now. Not while she was working. Besides, she knew who it was. Matt. Her boyfriend. The same as the last seventeen text messages and nine voicemail messages he'd left, blowing up her phone for the last hour and a half.

It was late afternoon on Christmas Eve. She was at the Easton Town Center mall. The shopping center was a mixed-use indoor and outdoor shopping mecca on the outskirts of Columbus, Ohio.

She sat on a bench outside. It was cold. A Christmas tree decorated with blue lights and a white star topper towered over the town square. A group of costumed carolers stood on Townsfair Way and sang "Silent Night." Mostly shoppers hurried by and paid little attention, their full bags rustling, banging against their legs, often deep in conversation or texting on their phones.

Rebecca sang along under her breath.

The sky had grown dark with the approaching evening. A gentle snow had begun to fall.

Festive, Rebecca thought approvingly, even as she shivered as the air grew chillier. She pulled the faux fur collar of her winter coat up around her neck and jammed her wool-gloved hands into the pockets of her coat. With her legs crossed, she bobbed one leg, hoping the movement would keep her warm. Thank goodness for her wool-lined Uggs. At least her toes were warm and toasty.

Rebecca's phone buzzed again.

153

Again, she ignored it. Matt couldn't understand why she had to work on Christmas Eve. It wasn't civilized, he complained. No one works on Christmas Eve.

What about the clerks in all the retail stores, dummy?

"It's a supervised visit with his kid," Rebecca had tried to explain. "And it's Christmas. It would be heartless to not let him see his little girl on Christmas Eve."

Rebecca was a case worker for the Ohio Public Children Services Agency, the state's child protective services. She was at the mall because one of her kids—she thought of them all as her kids—had a scheduled supervised visit with her father.

"The man's a criminal and junkie," Matt complained.

"He should still be able to see his daughter on Christmas Eve," Rebecca had argued. Not that she had any choice in the matter. The visitation was court-ordered. There wasn't anything Rebecca could do about it, even if she wanted to.

Which she did not, as she emphatically told Matt earlier in the day.

Across from where she sat, she could see the pink winter coat Jessie Armento wore with its white fur trim. She and her dad, Patrick, stood in a small crowd listening to the carolers sing. They'd moved on to "Away in the Manger."

Jessie was a cute and funny nine-year-old. She had long brown hair that she'd asked Rebecca to tie into two cute ponytails. One tied off with a red ribbon, the other with a green one.

For Christmas, she'd said. For Daddy.

In addition to the belted pink coat, she wore a white wool hat with dangling pompoms and matching wool mittens. She stood listening to the singers with her back to Rebecca, her arm clutched around a well-loved, soiled white bear she'd named—appropriately enough—Teddy.

She also held her daddy's hand.

Rebecca didn't think much of him. A gangly man with hard breath. Thin. He had ugly pock-scarred cheeks. His long brown hair was greasy and unkempt. His eyes were always bloodshot and watery. Tonight, he had on a blue denim jacket.

154

It was soiled at the elbows. He wore baggy gray pants and scuffed-up Timberland boots.

Under his knuckles, he had prison-inked tattoos on each finger. K-I-L-L on one hand. P-I-G-S on the other. Rebecca had spotted the needle mark scars between his fingers where he'd shot up when he used. He had cleared a pee test that morning, but that didn't relieve Rebecca's concerns.

She knew Patrick had a long criminal record. Drugs and burglaries mostly, and at least two grand theft auto charges. He was out on bail for larceny, possession of a class A substance, and endangerment of a child. He'd been doing drugs in his car, with Jessie in the backseat.

Rebecca wondered if maybe Matt wasn't right. Maybe people like Patrick Armento didn't deserve a second chance. Hadn't he—people like him—thumbed their noses at their rights by continuing their despicable conduct? What else had he exposed his child to? What if she'd been hurt? What if she'd needed help while he was…incapacitated? Incapable?

Rebecca shook her head. No. Everyone deserved a second chance. The benefit of the doubt. Either way, it wasn't for her to say. Besides, this was as much for Jessie as it was the father, wasn't it? The girl deserved to know her father. To see for herself the sort of man he really was.

Her phone buzzed again.

"Jesus, Matt, give it a rest." She pulled the phone out of her pocket.

Behind her, she heard the clip-clop of horses' hooves on the street's pavement. She turned. It came from the holiday carriage rides around the mall. A family was in the white carriage: a mother and father, two little girls. They were laughing and smiling, surrounded by stuffed, colorful shopping bags. The driver, in a top hat, clucked at the two big white horses.

Rebecca's phone—now in her hand—buzzed again.

She went to look at it, but the device slipped from her mitten-covered hand. The phone clattered to the cobblestone pavement. "Oh, shoot…"

Rebecca grabbed it off the wet pavement, wiped the screen, and angrily stabbed at the connect button with the nanotip piece of her mitten. She put the phone to her ear. "Damn it, Matt, I told you—"

She stopped mid-sentence, scanning the crowd around the carolers, looking for Patrick and Jessie Armento…and not seeing them! "Shit!"

In her ear, she heard Matt's voice. "Rebecca. Rebecca!"

She called out, "Jessie!"

Rebecca pushed through the crowd, shoving people out of her way as she moved toward where she last saw Jessie and her father. The carolers sang "Jingle Bells."

"Jessie! Jessie!"

"Hey, watch it!" a man carrying a wrapped over-size box shouted.

"You watch it," Rebecca shouted back. "Jessie! Mr. Armento! Where are you?"

She ran around the carolers, looked up and down Townsfair Way, then south down Easton Square Place, calling out the whole time. The crowd of people seemed to get larger, thicker. Impenetrable. A swirling sea of people around her.

What had she done?

Jessie and Patrick Armento were nowhere to be seen.

Rebecca pushed back through the crowd, retraced her steps.

There.

On the ground, she found something.

She pushed against the jostling crowd around her to pick it up. Soaking wet. A teddy bear. Teddy.

She looked around again. Jessie…

But the girl was gone. Jessie was gone!

I PULLED MY Jeep to the curb on Broad Street in front of Large Louie Gravelle's seedy little bail bondsman storefront. The place was in West Columbus, a basically crummy part of town. Be where your clients are. That's a business motto, isn't it?

His place was part of a cluster of commercial real estate buildings that were mostly closed businesses. The pawn shop still operated. But that was kept afloat by the city's brisk black market stolen property trade. There was also a dance club on the corner. It only operated on weekends. I suspected the drug trade kept them in business.

Even though it was late Saturday afternoon, it was Christmas Eve, so the beat of bass-heavy rap that usually thumped from the place was absent. The streets were deserted. The pavement was wet with melted snow. A few flurries fell.

I pulled the door to his place open. The bell overhead rang, announcing my arrival.

Louie's storefront inside matched its surroundings outside. Namely, it was a dump. The front half had a large round table, scarred and with one bent leg that Louie kept propped up with a telephone book. Where he'd gotten his hands on a telephone book in this day and age was a mystery to me. The carpet was perpetually soggy. A dozen mismatched chairs lined the walls for his clients to use. They were written on with magic markers, stained, and dotted with cigarette burns.

"Your fat ass better be on fire, Louie," I said, storming across the space. "It's Christmas Eve and Suzie's talked me into having a holiday party—"

"Tell your darkie friend to get lost." This came from a woman standing next to Louie, where he sat at his desk in the

157

employee-only section behind the storefront counter. She held a knife to this throat.

"Tell her you ain't taking on no new clients at the moment," the woman said to Louie.

The woman was skinny as a scarecrow with a druggie's smudged, hollow eyes. They were a brown and listless. Her hair was dishwater blond. She wore a thin gray hoodie. It was a size too big, so it hung off her frame.

What the hell was this?

"This isn't a client," Louie said. His beady eyes darted from the woman's face to her hand at his throat. "She's the one I told you about."

I approached the swing gate that separated the client area from the employee area. "I don't know what's going on here."

"So turn around and take your skinny black ass outta here."

"Okay, first off, I'm not black. I'm a wonderful blend of Latina and Irish. That's what gives me this beautiful dusky skin. So, not black." I pushed through the swing gate. "As for skinny? Girl, you've got some nerve."

"Don't come in here."

Too late. I was in already. "Secondly, the next thing out of your ugly, racist mouth better be an apology. Otherwise, we're going to have a real problem."

"Stay back." The woman jabbed the knife into Louie's jowly neck, drawing a dollop of blood.

"Grace," he squawked.

"I'm armed three ways to Sunday," I said, ignoring Louie. "So I bet I can kill you before you can slit his throat." I flipped my leather coat open to reveal the holstered .45 I had on my left hip. "Wanna put money on it?"

"Grace," Louie pleaded. "This isn't the time to be making wagers."

"Or," I said, giving the woman a second choice. "You can put the knife down and tell me what the fuck's going on here?"

The woman took her time sizing me up, but then she pulled the knife away from Louie. She took a step back. Louie gasped and leaned forward, grabbing his throat. His hand disappeared under the rolling layers of fat that were his chin.

He rolled his chair away from the woman. "Grace, I called you because Stephanie...her daughter's been kidnapped by her ex-boyfriend."

"Common law husband," she said and spit.

I looked from her to him. "Okay. So?"

She pointed an accusing finger at Louie. "He put up Patrick's bail. It's 'cause of him Patrick's out. And now...now my baby's gone."

Worked up again, she raised the knife and stepped toward Louie.

He scooted away like a little bitch. The wheels on his chair protested loudly. That they hadn't snapped carrying all that weight surprised me.

I grabbed Stephanie's arm, stopping her.

"Why call me?" I directed the question at Louie.

"Yeah?" She wanted to know, too.

"This is Grace deHaviland," Louie said. "She can help you."

"Me help her?" I said, with my eyebrow arched in Louie's direction. "I don't do kidnappings, Louie, or help racist junkies."

Louie's pointed bald head shimmered with sweat. I've freelanced for him for quite a few years. He and I were not, nor would we ever be, friends. With beady eyes, he looked at me from under drooping eyebrows, pleading with me to help him.

Stephanie shook a cigarette from a crumbled pack. She scissored it between two fingers and lit it with the flick of a lighter. She squeezed one eye closed against the curl of smoke. "He says you're supposed to be some whiz-bang bounty hunter."

The woman sank into a chair next to Louie's desk. The knife remained in her hand.

On his desk was an open box. At one time in the recent past, it had held Christmas cookies. The only thing left was red and green sugar dust and a single decapitated Santa's head.

"He told me," the woman continued, "not to worry. Patrick won't jump bail. He put his mom's trailer up for collateral. No one would run away and let their mom lose her home." She barked a harsh laugh. "He sure don't know Patrick."

After another drag on her cigarette, she stared hot daggers at Louie. "All you cared about was getting your hands on the money."

That sounded like the Louie I knew.

"I explained," Louie said, "if Patrick did jump bail, it wouldn't be a problem."

Stephanie slammed her hand down on the desk. "It is a problem! He took my girl. He took my little Jessie!"

"I couldn't have—"

Another loud slap on the desk cut him off.

"You should have." Stephanie looked at me. "He said he had the best bounty hunter in the business working for him. He said she can find anyone, anywhere." Stephanie stood up. "That's you, isn't it?"

"You said that?" I asked Louie. "You think I'm the best in the business."

It was an undeniable fact. I was just surprised to hear Louie admit it.

He shrugged. "It was a sales pitch."

"Bastard."

"Stop it!" Stephanie shouted. "This is about my Jessie. My little baby."

"You're right," I said. "Look, I want to help. I really do." No, I didn't. "But like you said, I'm a bounty hunter, and Patrick hasn't jumped bail. Missed any court appointments." Which was true. I looked at Louie. "Has he?"

He shook his head. His jowls jiggled. Red and green sugar granules were caked wetly at the corners of his thin mouth. Ugh.

"Then this is a matter for the police." I turned and headed for the swing gate.

"Wait," Stephanie cried out. "They're already involved, but they're not telling me nothing."

"It was a court-ordered visitation," Louie said.

"What does that mean?" I asked.

"That…technically…it could be classified as a failure to appear," he said.

"No, it can't," I said. "Bullshit." Not sure, I asked, "Right?"

"An argument could be made." He shrugged. "He's got a court appearance scheduled for Tuesday, just two days after Christmas. What do you wanna bet he doesn't show up for that?"

I didn't answer.

Stephanie stared at me.

"Think of it as getting a head start," Louie suggested.

Fuck you, I thought. But I said, "You have his bail papers?"

What I wanted to ask was how much the bond was. But given the circumstances, that seemed a little tacky.

He picked up a file and held it out to me.

I snatched it from him and flipped it open.

Inside was the usual. Arrest record. Basic background information. List of court appearances. A five-by-seven-size copy of his mugshot, suitable for framing. Bail was set at fifty-thousand. That meant I'd earn five grand if I brought him in. But if I found him before he actually jumped bail, would I be entitled to the money? Was I being insensitive?

Probably not, and definitely yes, in that order.

"Does that mean you'll go get him?" Stephanie asked. "You'll bring my little girl back to me?"

I looked from her to Louie. He shrugged. "It's Christmas."

I mouthed the word: asshole. To Stephanie, I said, "Tell me what happened."

When she finished her story, I left.

Kidnap your own kid on Christmas Eve. How messed up was that?

Outside I pulled out my cell, hit the first number in my speed dial, and put the phone to my ear. "Suzie, I need some help."

CHAPTER TWO

"WHERE ARE YOU?" Suzie asked from the other end of the phone.

I stepped off the curb onto the wet pavement of West Broad Street. I waited for a couple of cars to speed past, then climbed in behind the wheel of my Jeep. "Large Louie's."

"Not the first person I'd expect to be on your Christmas card list," she said, followed by a pause. "Oh, no, Grace. No, no, no, no. You did *not* take on a case. It's Christmas Eve."

I shivered under my quilt-lined anorak-style leather coat.

I turned the heater on full blast, but it would be hard-pressed to do much against the Wrangler's plastic windows and the soft-shell top. I needed to get a suitable replacement for my Firebird. The car had been firebombed over the summer. It still broke my heart. It's probably why I hadn't dealt with it yet.

My silence betrayed me.

"Oh, Grace." I could hear the disappointment in her voice.

"It won't take long. It's an easy one, I promise." Of course, I had no idea how easy or hard the case would be. But, the thought of letting my best friend—my only friend—down tugged at my heart and gave me a sour feeling in my stomach.

"You've got a loft full of people here."

Surprised, I pulled out into the light stream of traffic, traveling east toward downtown. My wipers—set on slow intermediate—were enough to combat the falling snow. "*Why* do I have a loft full of people?"

"Your Christmas party. To decorate the tree."

"I don't have a tree."

"You do now. It's gorgeous. It's like twenty-five feet tall. Book and a couple of his guys from work put it up."

163

She sounded so excited.

I sighed. "When you said a tree-trimming party, I thought you meant you and me and Book, maybe a few others. And a Charlie Brown Christmas tree. Not a Rockefeller Center tree."

"Well, that's all it is. Really. It's not a lot."

"How many?" I asked with attitude.

"Only a handful of deputies could make it. From five or six surrounding counties."

"Suzie."

"A bunch of Columbus cops," she went on. "Book's entire team. Oh, and a few people from the courthouse, the bailiffs—"

"Stop."

"No, it's true. Tolman's here, too." My former CO when I was a sheriff's deputy. "Liz." Liz Vasco, a defense attorney who'd recently helped me beat a murder conviction. "And like her entire staff."

"No, I mean it, Suzie. Stop. I don't care who's there. They're all there for you, not me. None of 'em will even notice I'm not there."

"That's not true."

It was, and we both knew it. Those people were all friends of Suzie and Book, there for the free booze. None of them were my friends except Suzie and Book. And Tolman, sometimes. Depending on the level of trouble I'm causing him at the moment.

"Suzie, it's a child abduction case. Happened this afternoon at Easton. A parental-custodial thing. The girl's name is Jessie. The father is Patrick Armento. I need to know who caught the case."

"Hold on a minute."

I heard muted sounds. Distant conversations. Christmas Carols in the background. Laughing. Someone singing off-key. Very off-key. A minute passed as the downtown skyline came into view ahead of me. The buildings were lit up bright with red and green lights for Christmas. The street lamps were decked out with green garland. Snow flurries continued to fall. Pretty but melting on contact with the pavement and my windshield. The colorful lights sparkled off the surface of the Scioto River.

The wipers made a single streaky pass and plopped down.

Suzie returned to the line. "Tolman says Tom Harington's running point for the Sheriff's Office. A Detective Frank Abel caught the case for Columbus. They've issued an Amber Alert."

Harington, I knew. He was a good man. I didn't know the Columbus cop.

"Thanks, girlfriend."

"Where are you? I'm coming to meet you."

"No," I said. "I'll let you know if I need anything else."

"Grace."

"I've got this." I disconnected from her and called the Sheriff's Office. I asked to speak to Harington.

I knew Tom from my days as a deputy. I doubted I'd ever consider Harington a friend, but he always gave me the benefit of the doubt during the trouble I went through there. That hadn't been the case with most of the other deputies.

"Harington," I said when I got him on the phone. "This is Grace deHaviland."

A pause. Then: "Yes?"

Cautious and frosty.

"I'm working the Armento case."

"He's a kidnapper, not a bail jumper."

"Not yet. But we can argue that later. I want to help. For the sake of the girl. Jessie."

Another pause. "What do you want?"

"Where does it stand?" I asked. "I know there's an Amber Alert, and you're working with Abel from Columbus." I made it sound like I knew him. "Has the alert turned up anything yet? Do you have any other leads?"

The line was quiet for so long I thought I'd been disconnected. Then Harington said, "We've talked with the case worker who lost them. We know it's the dad took her, Patrick Armento. The only lead we've got is from a witness.

Saw them get into his dark green Honda minivan behind the Barnes & Noble."

He paused, then added, "We've got a BOLO out for it in addition to the Amber Alert. Statewide. So far, no hits."

"Tell me about the parents."

I had the file Louie gave me open on the seat next to me. I eased to a stop at a red light and glanced at it. The mug shot of Patrick Armento stared back at me.

"A twenty-eight-year-old waste of space. A white supremacist and junkie who's been in and out of jail since he was sixteen. He's out on bail waiting for a third-strike drug possession and trafficking sentence."

A third-strike beef meant serious time. "He's got nothing to lose."

"Except his kid. The stretch he's facing must've made him desperate enough to pull a stupid stunt like this."

Desperate and stupid. Not a good combination. "What about the old lady?"

"Another prize."

"Tell me about it. When I met her, she called me a darkie and said I had a skinny black ass."

"She still breathing?" Harington asked.

I smiled. I guess my badass rep was still intact. "Didn't feel right killing her on Christmas Eve, not with her girl missing."

"You ain't going soft, are you, deHaviland?"

"Hell, no. Just don't want to do all that paperwork on Christmas?"

Harington continued, "Steph, as she's called. The two of them have been attached at the hip since they were caught boosting booze from a liquor store in the Bottoms in the seventh grade."

"Any thoughts she's a part of this? She did seem pretty broken up over it all."

"Not from what we can tell. Spoke to her aunt, Steph's mother's sister, and to the little girl's grandmother, Patrick's mom. They tell us the two had a falling out a few years back when Steph started turning tricks to support her habit while

Patrick was in the joint. One of them said—can't remember which one—she also used the money to pay his bail. Guess he didn't appreciate the effort."

"No good deed goes unpunished."

"Sounds like. He beat the shit out of her. Put her in the hospital with a couple of cracked ribs and a busted nose."

"Love hurts," I said.

"I guess," Harington agreed.

"The girl. She lives with either of these upstanding parental role models?"

"Naw. The system took her away. She lives in a foster home. The parents only get limited, supervised visitation, which brings us to where we are now."

"Foster home?" I said absently. "You got the address?"

THREE

TEN MINUTES LATER, I pulled up to a pleasant-looking colonial in Upper Arlington, one of the more upscale communities in central Ohio. The house was well-maintained, freshly painted in a pretty shade of aqua-marine blue with green trim. Being a little farther north of downtown, the lawn had a scrim of snow on it, in contrast to the dark pavement of the driveway and the street where the falling snow melted on contact.

The yard was festooned with lights and Christmas stuff. An inflatable snow globe dominated the yard. Inside, it was the North Pole with pretend snow billowing around inside. I could hear the low hum of an unseen generator forcing air through it, keeping the snow inside in a constant state of yuletide swirl. On the other side of the sidewalk leading up to the wide front porch was an inflatable Santa in a sled being pulled by eight tiny reindeer. They trembled as the pump blew a steady flow of hot air into them.

The door to the house opened as I approached. I'd called ahead.

Mrs. Knowles shook my hand with a solid grip.

Stocky and in her mid-sixties, her short brown hair was streaked with gray. Her dark eyes were bright and sharp. She led me to the kitchen table and made me a cup of coffee. The kitchen smelled of fresh-baked cookies. My stomach grumbled, hoping she'd offer me something.

"Call me Helen," she said, joining me. "You're really a bounty hunter? I didn't know that was a real thing?"

"It is." I slid my card across the table to her.

She picked it up. Examining it, she flicked the edge of the card with her thumb. "Always thought it was something made up for them TV cop shows."

"Nope. We're real."

"Must be exciting."

"It has its moments." I took a sip of coffee. "I'm here to get some background information on Jessie and her parents, specifically her dad, Patrick Armento."

Helen gave me a sour expression. "A most disagreeable man. Arrogant and angry." She huffed. "Like he's got something to be superior about. In and out jail since he was a teenager. On the drugs. Bad. It's got its hooks into him. He can't shake it loose."

"He trying?"

"Not really. Been to all the court-ordered groups and whatnot. He's just doing what he's got to, to get out of whatever predicament he's gotten himself into. I'm sure you know how it is, being in your line of work. It's not going to take 'less they want it to."

She shook her head like it was a shame.

I guessed it was.

"From what I've seen in the file, it looks like he's facing a pretty long prison sentence."

Helen nodded. "That's what his caseworker told me, too."

"You weren't worried about him visiting with Jessie?"

"Course, it worried me. That girl's been through so much in her short time on this Earth. Breaks my heart. Comes back torn up each time after seeing one of them. She's conflicted."

"How do you mean?"

"She's his daughter. She wants to love her daddy, probably does, but she's afraid of him. Scares her."

"You think he'd hurt her? Is he violent?"

"No, not like that. Scares her the way he is. Loud. Curses all the time. Scruffy. Those tattoos on his hands and his neck."

The "kill pigs" finger tats were recorded on his arrest sheet. There was no mention of a neck tattoo.

She tapped the side of her neck. "A shamrock with the number six on each leaf. 666. That's the devil's mark, isn't it? And letters. An A and a B in gothic letters."

"Aryan Brotherhood." I thought back to Stephanie's darkie comment to me. Birds of a feather. As a former sheriff's deputy and having worked inside prisons, I knew the Aryan Brotherhood made up less than one percent of the prison population, but they were responsible for over twenty percent of all the murders committed on the inside. A dangerous bunch.

A very dangerous association.

"They're the ones spew all that anti-black, anti-Semite stuff, right? Yeah, that sounds like Patrick." She shook his head. "He's got ugly opinions about people. Kills me to let Jessie get exposed to that kind of thinking."

"You've been a foster parent long?"

She smiled warmly. "My whole adult life. John, my husband, and me. We couldn't have children of our own. We thought about adopting, but when we heard about all these kids who were in trouble. We thought wouldn't it be wonderful if we could help a bunch of kids instead of just one or two."

"That sounds very generous of you."

Again, she smiled. "We never took on more than two or three of the little darlings at a time. We wanted to give them our undivided attention. Make it as close to a real family experience as we could. Besides, some of them could be a handful, as you can imagine."

"Mr. Knowles. Is he around so I might talk to him, too?"

"Oh, John passed, going on six years now. Cancer."

"I'm sorry."

"He had a good life." She looked wistfully off into the distance. "We had a good life," she amended. "It's why I keep fostering kids. It's what he would have wanted." She gave a short laugh. "It keeps me on my toes. I will tell you that."

"How many kids do you have?"

"Just Jessie for now. I felt like she needed a little extra attention, considering her situation."

"I understand."

"Do you think she's going to be okay?" Helen put her hand on my arm. "Tell me straight. These sorts of things. How often do they turn out okay? You know, for the child?"

I patted her arm. "Parental custody cases are the sort least likely to bring harm to the child. Generally, the parent does what they do because they care about the child, out of love, not because they wish them harm. That's in our favor."

"But," Helen said, reading the concern on my face. "You have concerns. Don't you lie to an old woman, you hear me?"

"I wouldn't dare." I gave her a reassuring smile. "Armento doesn't have a history of violence, but he is the subject of a massive manhunt. He's facing a very long sentence, maybe life, even before this stunt. There'll be additional charges when this is all over. If he crosses state lines, that'll bring federal kidnapping charges into it. The FBI. And he's got ties to the Aryan Brotherhood. They're not known for giving up easily."

"Jessie could be caught up in all of that."

"That's what I'm hoping to avoid."

"What makes you think you can find them when the police haven't?"

"Because I'm better than they are."

Helen gave me a skeptical look.

"I don't say that because I'm full of myself or I'm conceited." Which I'm often accused of being. It's not being conceited if it's true, I reminded myself. "This is what I do for a living. I need to be good at it, or I don't eat."

"I see."

"Would you mind if I take a look at Jessie's room?"

"Of course not." Helen stood up. "If you think it'll help."

CHAPTER FOUR

JESSIE'S ROOM WAS what you might expect for a nine-year-old girl. There was eggshell white wallpaper with dancing ballerina bears holding pink and blue balloons. A hand-painted red chest of drawers with a matching mirror over it. The frame was bedazzled with colorful, sparkling stickers. There was a child-size writing desk under the window. A princess castle at the foot of the bed. On it were Cinderella bedspread and sheets.

I had no idea what I hoped to find here.

"Are you ever present during her supervised visits with either of the parents?" I asked Mrs. Knowles, who loomed in the doorway. Watching me.

"Only when Jessie makes them come here for their visits. I think she feels comfortable here, feels safe here." She said it with great pride in her voice. "The agency tells me I have to leave, but I tell them no. I won't be chased from my house by those...people. I leave them alone, but I stay."

I smiled. I liked the feisty older woman.

"Have you ever overheard Patrick or Stephanie talk about family or friends? The kind of people they might rely on to hide them or help them leave town?"

She pursed her lips, thinking, but slowly shook her head. "No. They're not exactly the chatty type. I can't imagine any folks who'd invite them home for Sunday dinner if you know what I mean."

"I do."

I gave the room a final look, thinking I'd learned as much as I was going to—which wasn't much at all—when I noticed the wastepaper basket next to the small desk. It was half full

172

of balled-up red and white papers, the same as a pad sitting on the desk.

Christmas-themed stationery. A box of crayons next to it.

"Did Jessie write a letter to Santa recently?" I asked, walking over to the desk.

"Yes. Last week."

"Do you still have it?"

"No. We mailed it. Put it into the little red Santa mailbox outside the post office."

I picked up the wastepaper basket and dumped the crumpled papers out on the desk. I returned the wastebasket to the floor and pawed through the papers. I unwrinkled papers, smoothing them out on the surface of the desk. Each was written in crayon, some in red, and some in green. Each began with "Dear Santa" in the childlike penmanship of a nine-year-old.

Seven pages in all. Discarded early attempts.

"Did you read it?" I asked, meaning the letter.

"No. She didn't show it to me. I didn't think…."

I waved off her second guessing. "No reason you should have."

From reading the various first attempts, I got a pretty good idea of what went into the final draft. I read out loud what I'd pieced together from the crumpled letters.

Dear Santa,

This is Jessie Armento. I hope everything is nice in the North Pole and it is not too cold. I hate the cold. I do not want toys or dolls or anything like that this year for Christmas. All I want is for mommy and daddy to be off drugs and not be so angry. They scare me sometimes.

Momma tells me one day she'll be better and we'll go to a cabin on a lake in the woods. The way she talks about it it sounds nice. She says we can go live there. Go swimming and be in a boat and go fishing. Her and Daddy and me.

It sounds like a nice place. But I don't want to go there, Santa. Not to live. Not with them. Not the way they are. I love mommy and daddy but they scare me.

Please, Santa, all I want for Christmas is for mommy and daddy to let me stay here. And so you know, when I say here I mean here with Mrs. Knowles. If that can happen it'll be the best Christmas ever. And, I'll be a good girl forever.

Love, Jessie

P.S. I know I said I didn't want any toys and stuff. But a puppy! That would be awesome. I would love it and play with it and take care of it forever. I promise.

Mrs. Knowles sat on the edge of the bed, tears rolling down her cheeks. Her bottom lip trembled, which she covered with her hand. When she looked up, she said, "Do you think...."

"Did you ever hear anyone talk about a cabin? A lake? Anything like that?"

"No. Wait, yes." She looked up, hopeful. "Not about going there, but yes. It was back during the summer. Jessie and Stephanie were outside at the picnic table. Jessie asked me to prepare a picnic lunch for them. I brought out sandwiches and drinks, and chips. Stephanie was talking about a cabin on a lake. I thought it was a story from when she was a little girl. I didn't think anything about it."

"Did she say anything about where it was? Think. Anything."

The woman looked away as she wiped tears from her face. Her focus was on the carpet. As if she might find the answers she wanted within the pattern of colorful alphabet squares in uppercase and lowercase letters.

Suddenly she snapped her head up. "Michigan!"

"How do you know? She said something?"

"No. It was another time. With Patrick. He was telling Jessie how he used to go fishing when he was young. On a lake in Michigan with his cousin."

"This cousin, does he have a name?"

She smiled triumphantly. "Pete. He called him Cousin Pete. I should have put it together."

"No. You had no way of knowing. Don't beat yourself up." I patted her arm. "You've been very helpful."

She grabbed my hand and squeezed it tightly. "You're going to find her, aren't you? You're going to find Jessie and bring that little girl home."

I squeezed back. "I'll do my best."

I started to leave, excited by what I'd learn, but Helen Knowles called out.

"Ms. deHaviland? One more thing." Helen grabbed a small white teddy bear sitting on Jessie's bed. It looked recently cleaned but in bad shape, or as Mom would've said, well-loved. "This is Teddy. He's Jessie's favorite. She doesn't go anywhere without him, but she must have dropped him when," she choked up, "at the mall."

She pressed it into my hand. "You make sure she gets Teddy back."

I took him with a tight squeeze. "I will. You have my word."

CHAPTER FIVE

BACK IN THE Jeep, I called Harington. "Anything on the BOLO or Amber Alert?"

"A lot of sightings. Nothing that's panned out," he told me. "Tell me you've got something."

The snow had picked up.

Driving away, I felt the tires slip a little. Snow was beginning to stick to the surface of the road. I slowed and relayed to Harington what I'd learned.

When I finished, I said, "We need to rethink Stephanie's involvement in all this. I'm on my way to her place now. If I'm right, she'll be gone."

"What about your encounter with her at the bail bonds place?"

"I don't know. An act, maybe. Throw suspicion off herself if she acted like a hysterical, overwrought mother."

"You really think they're together, heading for this cabin?"

"It's all we've got. I'll call you if I find anything, but it might not hurt to add Steph and her car to the alerts."

"Roger that," Harington said. "In the meantime, I'll see if we can track down Cousin Pete and his fishing hole."

Twenty minutes later, I learned I was right. Stephanie wasn't home. Neither was her car. A ten-year-old silver Sonata. Looked like the unhappy couple had reconciled after all.

Her mother, Fiona, who came to the door when I knocked, wasn't inclined to help locate her daughter or granddaughter if the nickel-plated Saturday Night Special she pointed at my face was any indication.

Should I have any doubt about that, they were erased as I backed away from the open door, my hands raised in the air, and she spat a wad of chewing tobacco on the tobacco-stained stoop.

"Get off my property. Fucking cops!"

I left without clarifying I wasn't the cops.

Pretty sure it wouldn't've made a difference.

I pulled down the street so as to not antagonize Stephanie's mother any more than I already had. A half block away, I stopped and reported back to Harington. I had nothing to add, but he'd been productive. He'd tracked down both Cousin Pete and the cabin.

Peter was Peter Lang. Patrick's mother's sister's son from a second marriage.

The cabin belonged to Pete's dad, who'd been accidentally shot to death on a hunting trip in Canada a few years after Pete was born. The two families would summer at the cabin when the boys were kids.

"Where is this cabin?" I asked.

"In Michigan. A place called Higgins Lake. Way the hell up north in the middle of the state. We've contacted the state police and the local county sheriff's office. They're sending a couple of uniforms out there to see what's what. They weren't pleased about it, it being Christmas Eve and all. I told them about Jessie, and it mollified them a little."

"How long's the drive from here to this Higgins Lake?"

"Six hours, in good conditions. The guy I talked to said there's a storm between us and them, dumping three inches of snow an hour. He said they've got roads closed along the way. Unless our guy got through before the bulk of that hit, he wasn't going to get anywhere."

It had only been about six hours since Jessie and Patrick disappeared. Not enough time to get to the cabin yet. That meant they were somewhere in between.

"Good news for us," I said. "They should still check out the cabin, see if Cousin Pete or any of his family's there."

"That's what I told him."

"Which leaves us to look at the roads between here and there. If the snow's as bad as they're saying—it's picking up here, that's for sure—the backroads will be impassable soon. If they're not already."

"Means they're going to have to stick with the major highways," Harington agreed.

"Which you've got covered."

His hesitation worried me.

When he spoke, it wasn't good news. "As best as we're able. We're short-staffed. It's Christmas Eve, after all. State police are doing what they can, but their hands are full with all the idiots on the roads spinning out and getting into accidents. We've reached out to the other sheriff's departments between here and the border, but like I said, short-staffed."

"It's a little girl, Harington!"

"I know that," he snapped back. "You think I don't know that? Why do you think I'm here and not at home with my family?"

I bit back a retort. Of course, he knew it. "I…let's just find them, okay?"

"I'll let you know if I hear anything."

"Thanks." But by the time I said it, he'd already hung up. Crap.

I cranked the Jeep's heater up to high. The fan blew out hot air. It wasn't sufficient to do battle with the dropping temperatures outside. Cold leaked in through the Jeep's plastic windows and fabric top. I seriously needed to put some thought into getting a new ride.

My cell rang. Suzie. I answered. "Hey."

"Hey."

"How's the party?"

"Be better if you were there. Since it's, you know, your place."

"Yeah." The thought of my warm, cozy loft and a cold beer, maybe something a little stronger, sounded like heaven. The windshield wipers squeaked, cleared snow from the glass, and thumped down to their resting position.

"I'm still going to be a while," I said.

"You're not at some dive bar, are you?"

"Jesus, no. Why would you even think that?"

"Because I invited all these people over, and you don't—"

"Like people," I finished for her. "No. That's not it."

"You're still working that Amber Alert case," she said.

"I've got a lead." As I spoke with Suzie, I pulled Higgins Lake, Michigan, up on my GPS and scrolled through the directions. The most direct route was US 75 toward Toledo. After that, the better part of three hours, going north on Route 23.

"What lead?" Suzie asked.

"There's a cabin in Michigan. I think that's where they're going."

"You're going to Michigan, aren't you?" Suzie asked, but it wasn't really a question.

I waited before saying yes.

I turned with a start as someone knocked on the passenger side frame of the Jeep.

Suzie pulled open the door and slipped into the bucket seat. "I knocked so you wouldn't shoot me." She pocketed her cell and smiled. "You're not going anywhere without me."

She wore a three-quarter-length leather coat covered with brushed chrome buckles, snaps, and zippers. Her black jeans were a patchwork of various heavy metal band logos and album covers. She wore black military leather jump boots laced up the middle, her jeans tucked inside. She brushed wet snow from her short spiky blond hair.

"Not very seasonal," I said of her outfit.

"You kidding? Look." She indicated her boots. The laces were red and green.

"Okay," I said, unimpressed.

"Well, what about this?" She pulled open her coat and thrust out her chest like Super Girl, revealing her uniform as she rushes out to save the day in a single bound.

I burst out laughing.

Suzie had on the white and red, ugly-as-sin, cheer-meister sweater the Grinch wore in the Jim Carrey movie. The five points on the drooping yellow star on top of its sad-sack tree were blinking lights.

As I wiped tears from my eyes, I asked, "What are you doing here, girl?"

"Same as you, looking for a little girl on Christmas Eve. Harington told me you were here."

"But—"

She cut me off. "Did you really think we'd let you be out here all night by yourself?"

"We?"

"Everybody," Suzie said. "As soon as I told them what you were working on, they all jumped in to help."

"Help how?"

"They're out looking. Some driving around. Others are calling law enforcement friends, colleagues, putting the word out. Others are on social media, spreading the news."

"Suzie, I don't know what to say."

"Don't say anything. Drive. Let's just get this son of a bitch and save that little girl's Christmas."

CHAPTER SIX

WE DROVE NORTH toward Toledo.

I told Suzie my theory. Stephanie and Patrick were working together to kidnap their daughter. They were heading for the cabin on the lake in Michigan. They'd be forced to stay on the main roads because of the snow. Weigh the risk of BOLOs and Amber Alerts over spinning out and sliding into a ditch and freezing to death on some backroad in the middle of nowhere, which is pretty much all there was between Columbus and Toledo—nothing.

As we drove north, the snow picked up precipitously. I loved that word.

The wind swirled the thickening white flakes across the headlights and created sweeping drifts over the plowed highway, now covered in at least an inch of fresh snow.

We'd driven for an hour without seeing a single vehicle except for one state plow that passed us going in the opposite direction.

Along the way, Suzie remained on the phone, directing the search patterns of police and civilians alike. She also kept in contact with Harington. He informed us the Michigan State police and a couple of Roscommon County Sheriff's deputies had made their way to Pete Lang's cabin but found it empty.

"Looked to be closed down for the season, they said, like most of the properties up that way this time of the year," Harington said.

We were coming up on a tiny black dot on the map of a town called Cary. It was where US 23 turned into Route 15.

I slowed down after feeling the back wheels fishtail under us. We were already doing less than forty miles an hour. Visibility was getting worse. I flipped on the high beams, but it only made the falling, blowing snow brighter. And the black sky darker.

"Hey, flip the high beams on again," Suzie said.

I did.

"See that?" She pointed off to the left.

I squinted.

The road was covered with drifting snow. On either side were flat fields buried under a blanket of five or six inches of the white stuff. But just above the rolling bank of a drainage gully ahead, I saw what had caught Suzie's eye.

A faint blinking yellow light.

I slowed and steered across the road. About fifty feet ahead, off the embankment and under a couple of inches of snow, was what looked like the tail end of a spun-out minivan.

As we got closer, I eased the Jeep to a stop. It skidded a little before coming to a complete stop at a bit of an angle.

Neither of us wanted to get out, but I grabbed a large metal Maglite I kept stuffed between my seat and the door and flicked on the powerful beam.

"You can stay here," I offered.

"In for a penny." Suzie pulled out a white and red wool hat that matched her Grinch sweater and tugged it on her head. It had hanging fuzzy red pompoms. "In for a pound."

I laughed and said, "Come on."

With effort, I pushed the door open against the howling wind. The outside cold was bracing. The whipping snow stung my cheeks. We trudged along the road toward the van, angled downward in the gully.

As we got closer, I could tell the make and model. It was a Honda minivan.

Patrick Armento and Jessie were last seen getting into his dark green minivan.

I focused the flashlight on the license plate. It was covered with road sand and grit-encrusted snow. I couldn't read the numbers. I unbuttoned my coat—reluctantly—and extracted my .45.

Suzie did the same, pulling her Ladysmith revolver. She grasped it in both hands. She wore fingerless wool gloves. Smart.

My gloves were back in the Jeep. Idiot.

The minivan was covered with snow. The emergency flashers—one of which had caught Suzie's eye—glowed dully under a layer of snow each time they blinked on.

I circled around to the front of the passenger-side sliding door.

Suzie reached for the handle and pulled the door back. She slipped in the snow.

I swept the interior with my gun, but the vehicle was empty. "Clear."

As Suzie holstered her revolver, I brushed the snow from the license plate. It was Patrick's car.

Suzie climbed into the backseat and searched it but didn't find anything helpful.

Back in the Jeep, Suzie called Harington to tell him what we found. She put her phone on speaker.

"Any idea where they made off to?" he asked.

I held my wet, cold hands over the heater vent, hoping I'd be able to feel my fingertips soon.

"If they walked away, they couldn't have gone far," I said, making a fist and blowing warm air into it, then returning it to the heater.

"Stephanie could have been following in her car. They could be hours ahead of us," Suzie said. I knew what she was thinking. The storm had turned, it was getting worse, and we were driving straight into it.

"We can't go on much farther," I said.

Suzie grabbed my arm. She shook it. "Hey. You've done good. And we'll keep going for as long as we can."

"She's right, Grace," Harington said. "Thanks to you, we got a reasonable search area now. Concentrate our resources better."

He hung up, and we sat in the cold.

"Sorry about the party."

"No sweat. It's not like Jose Cuervo won't be there when we get back."

I put the car into gear and gingerly started down the road.

After a few minutes, I saw lights on the left. A sign for a chain hotel. And around it, a small cluster of restaurants, stores, and a gas station.

"We should start checking places they might have stopped at. Maybe they're somewhere waiting out the storm."

"Good idea," Suzie said.

I carefully aimed the Jeep for what looked like the hotel's entrance. "And I need to pee."

We bumped over something that felt like a curb but managed to pull into the parking lot without doing any damage. I breathed a sigh of relief, wondering at the wisdom of trying to continue on from here.

The lot had been paved at some point, probably more than once, but it looked like a couple of inches had fallen since the last pass. I counted seven cars parked in various spots along the front. All were under several inches of snow. They'd arrived earlier in the evening and hadn't moved since.

I drove past the front entrance and pulled around back. There were no cars along the side of the building. But, behind the hotel, we found three.

I tapped Suzie's shoulder and pointed at an old silver Sonata with a dented rear panel. "Our luck's just changed, girl. That's Stephanie's car."

"No way."

"Way. It's our own little Christmas miracle."

CHAPTER SEVEN

SUZIE STAYED IN the Jeep while I went inside. I used the facilities and then went looking for the manager on duty or anyone in charge.

The lobby was decorated with red and green streamers from which Merry Christmas, Ho Ho Ho, and Happy New Year hung in gold letters. Evergreen garland was wrapped around the banisters of the wide stairs that led to the second floor. There were tiny blinking lights everywhere.

In the large room where the hotel served its complimentary hot breakfast, there was a fireplace with a warm crackling fire. A large screen TV mounted above the firebox was tuned to a music station playing Christmas songs, and a thirty-foot tall Christmas tree complete with ornaments, tinsel, and wrapped presents around its base dominated the room.

Empty boxes, I assumed.

The carols playing on the TV were pumped softly through speakers throughout the lobby.

No one was at the registration desk when I got there. I rang the silver bell for service.

A plump black woman in her mid-thirties appeared from somewhere in the back. She smiled pleasantly. "Merry Christmas. How can I help you?"

I brushed snow off the arms of my leather coat. "I need to know if you've seen this man." I showed her Patrick Armento's mug shot. "He might have had a little girl with him. Nine years old. Dark hair. Wearing a pink coat."

She looked at the picture.

"Why are you looking for them? Are you a police officer?"

I pulled out my badge and ID. "I'm a bounty hunter. He's skipped bail."

"But it's Christmas Eve."

She seemed like a nice woman, but I was losing my patience. "Their car's outside. Did they come in for a room or not?"

"I'm not allowed to give out that information. It's against—"

"Listen," I looked at her name tag, "Malia. The little girl's been kidnapped. She could be in danger."

"How do I know you're telling me the truth?"

"So you have seen them?"

"I think you can trust her, Malia," said a voice from behind the Christmas tree.

A moment passed, the tree shook, and then Santa Claus backed out from behind the tree.

Yeah, my thought, too. No way.

But there he was. Fat guy in a red suit, shiny black boots, full white beard. He held a wrapped present in his gloved hand and smiled.

Where in the hell did he come from?

Didn't matter.

"Thanks, Santa." I would have used air quotes, but I hate people who use air quotes. "I've got this."

I returned my attention to Malia. "Look, call someone if you have to. Whatever. But I need to know where this guy is. Now."

"I could call the manager. He's at home."

"Then do it," I said.

"I don't mean to interrupt," Santa said, coming up beside me.

"Then don't," I snapped. "I've got enough problems as it is."

"I'm not trying to be a bother," he said. "But I think you're right. I think you need to act right away."

I turned on him. "I don't need your input…*Santa*."

"This is—"

I cut Malia off. "I don't care who he is—"

186

"I come around every year to visit the boys and girls who are traveling on Christmas," Santa said, cutting me off. "They get concerned Santa won't know where they are."

"It's nice," Malia said. "Suit looks real nice this year. Is it new?"

The old guy's cheeks turned apple-red. "This old thing, no—"

"Great. Cool and all." I snapped my fingers at Malia. "Manager. Phone. Now."

She went about looking for a card or call list or whatever so she could call her boss. I turned toward Santa. "What'd you mean I should act right away?"

"Your man came in earlier—"

"So they *are* here." I shot Malia a recriminating look.

With the phone to her ear, she turned her back on me.

To Santa, I said, "Go on."

"He was alone. I didn't see the girl. He had a shopping bag, probably from the Quickie-Mart across the way."

I'd noticed it when Suzie and I drove in.

"He also had two bottles of gin with him." Santa shook his head. "From the look of him, I'm not surprised he's on the naughty list."

I couldn't argue that. "Thanks."

Malia put the phone down.

"Well?" I urged.

"My manager's not home. I spoke to his babysitter. He's out at a holiday party. I tried his cell phone, but it went straight to voicemail. He's always letting the battery die on that thing."

"Damn it." I came around the counter.

Malia shied away from me. "What are you doing?"

I looked down at the counter. There was a keyboard and computer screen, but I was clueless as to what I thought I'd do back there. "Give me their room number and a key. Now!"

Malia jumped at my demand, but Santa gave her a reassuring nod. "Go on, Malia. It's the right thing to do."

She didn't look as if she agreed, but she tapped a few keys and swiped a card key through a machine. "Room 207."

She handed me the card key.

I took it. "Thank you."

I came out from around the counter. "Room 207. Where's that?"

"Up the main stairs here," Malia pointed, "Take a right down the hall. Third room on the left."

"That faces out on the front. Not the back, correct?"

"Yes," Malia confirmed.

"Perfect." I started for the steps, then stopped. "Oh, and call the police."

I bounded up the wide, carpeted steps to the second floor and called Suzie. I told her what I had in mind.

The corridor was empty. I found the elevators and the stairwells on either side. Once I had the lay of the land, I started to text Suzie back with the go-ahead. I stopped when the man playing Santa came bounding up the stairs.

"What are you doing?" I made no attempt to conceal my annoyance.

"I was curious as to your plan."

"Seriously?"

"I want to ensure no one gets hurt, especially Jessie."

"Me, too," I said. "And that includes you."

"Tell me your plan," he insisted.

Just what I didn't need: a Good Samaritan. But I decided it would be faster to tell him and get him on his way than to argue with him. "I've got a friend waiting in the parking lot. She's going to set off the car alarm. Get one of them to go out to shut it off."

"Separate them. That's good."

"Glad you approve," I said with all the snark I could muster.

He smiled, seemingly amused.

"Suzie'll take care of whichever one goes down. I'll hit the room and deal with the one that's left."

"I don't like it," Santa said.

"Excuse me?"

"He'll send the woman down."

How do you know….

"I know people like him. You'll need to deal with Patrick," Santa continued. "He's been drinking for an hour or more."

"I can handle him," I said.

"I don't doubt it, but even with the key, by the time you rush into the room…."

He let the statement hang before adding, "What if he puts that little security bar back in place? What if he's armed?"

"There's a good chance he is."

"He'll have the drop on you. Or worse, he'll grab the girl. You'll have a hostage situation to deal with." He gave me a stern look. That he looked like Santa, with a real beard and not a stuffed suit, like some cheap department store Santa, was disturbing. It was like getting scolded by the real Santa., to say the least.

"We both know those situations don't often end well."

"We do, do we?"

"You need to draw him out," Santa suggested.

"How do you suppose I do that? Look around. This isn't the kind of place that's got room service."

"I'll do it."

"Do what?"

"Draw him out." He wiped a white-gloved finger across his full red lips. "He saw me downstairs earlier. I'll knock. Tell him I've got a complimentary gift for his girl."

He fell silent while I mulled it over.

Before I could shoot the idea down, he said, "He'll see me in the peephole. Who's suspicious of seeing Santa Claus on Christmas Eve?"

I hated to admit it, but it could work.

CHAPTER EIGHT

I SENT SUZIE a text. *We're a go.*

From where Santa and I stood waiting by the stairs—yeah, I can't believe I said that either—we could hear the car alarm go off. Not loud, muffled by distance. Afraid Stephanie and Patrick wouldn't realize it was their car, I sent Santa down to have Malia ring the room. Tell them she'd received a complaint.

When Santa returned, he nodded. With that done, he offered me a reindeer-shaped sugar cookie with red sprinkles on it. I hadn't eaten in hours. It was pretty good.

A minute passed before we heard a door open.

"Just go shut the damn thing off." A male voice. "We can't afford no attention."

I counted to five and carefully looked around the corner.

Stephanie walked away from us, toward the far stairwell. She mumbled under her breath, shrugging into a heavy blue parka. She slammed through the stairwell door at the end of the corridor and went downstairs.

The door clicked closed behind her.

"Come on, Santa. You're up."

He walked with me to the door.

I could hear the TV playing inside. I stood beside the door and drew my weapon.

He looked at it with a disapproving frown.

I mouthed the word *go*.

Santa nodded and knocked on the door with his white gloved hand.

At first, there was no response. Santa knocked harder.

From inside, Patrick shouted, "Goddamn it! You forgot your damn room key, didn't you, you stupid bitch."

190

But there was a pause before he pulled the door open in anger. Probably he was peering through the fisheye. I could almost hear his stunned grunt seeing jolly old St. Nick standing on the far side of the peephole. As the seconds passed without word or action from Patrick, I worried he was getting suspicious. I rolled my hand in the air, indicating Santa should say something.

He cleared his throat. "Um, Merry Christmas."

I raised an eyebrow. *Go on.*

In a gregarious voice, he said, "I got word while on my travels that a little girl was far away from home tonight. I didn't want her to think I couldn't find her." He held up the cheerfully wrapped box he'd brought up from downstairs. "I wanted to make sure Jessie got her present from me tonight."

Had I told him Jessie's name?

I counted the seconds as they ticked by. Adrenaline pumped through my system. I worried this wasn't going to work. I fished for the card key in my pocket, preparing for plan B when the deadbolt snapped back.

I waved for Santa to back away from the door.

The security lock bar, as Santa called it, disengaged.

The deadbolt thudded open.

The door opened inward.

Come out. Just a step, I urged silently, tightening the grip on my .45.

First, the barrel of a rifle emerged. It was held casually at Patrick's side.

From inside the room, the TV played. Over the sound of a looney-tunes cartoon, a little girl called out, "Who is it, Daddy?"

Patrick took a step into the corridor.

He wore a grungy, once-white T-shirt and plaid boxer shorts. His chin sported two days of stubble, and his sandy brown hair was a riot of greasy spikes. Like he'd spent a lot of time running his hands through it.

I grabbed him by the front of his T-shirt and pulled. With surprise on my side, he stumbled forward, off-balance. Santa jumped out of the way. I spun Patrick around, slammed my forearm across his chest, and shoved him into the wall.

At the same time, I slapped the rifle away. It hit the carpeted floor with a thud.

He tried to grab my wrist.

I shifted my blocking arm until I had the barrel of the .45 drilled into the hollow space under his chin and his head pressed against the wall behind him.

I lowered my voice. "I don't want to splatter your brains all over this hallway in front of your kid on Christmas Eve, but so help me, I will if you make me."

His bulging, bloodshot eyes told me he believed me.

I pressed the barrel deeper, harder into his throat. "Nod, if you understand."

"I get it," he snarled. "Bitch." His breath was hard as kerosene.

I pulled him from the wall, hooked my leg around his ankles, and tripped him.

Patrick Armento crashed face first to the floor. I cuffed him behind his back without any more trouble. With my knee in the small of his back, I looked toward the hotel room.

"What's going on, Daddy? Daddy?" Jessie called out from inside the room.

She wandered toward the open door, dressed in a pair of Cinderella pajamas.

Santa stepped into the room and dropped to one knee, blocking her way, keeping her inside. "Merry Christmas, Jessie," Santa said with a hearty ho ho ho.

I called out, "Santa."

He looked over at me as Jessie Armento hugged him tightly. He patted her back.

From under my coat, I pulled out Teddy and tossed the bear to the jolly old man in red.

He caught Teddy and smiled, presenting him to the little girl.

"TEDDY!" Tears streaked her smudgy face. A mix of bad tears and good.

Yeah, there were tears in my eyes, too.

CHAPTER NINE

SUZIE HAD TAKEN Stephanie Armento into custody with little resistance. By the time I dragged Patrick Armento down to the lobby, with Jessie clinging tightly to Santa's leg and holding Teddy in a death grip, Harington and a dozen other cops from various agencies and jurisdictions had arrived.

We sat Patrick and Stephanie down in two chairs facing the Christmas tree. Both were handcuffed and looked anything but joyous on this holiday night.

The billowing snow outside had tapered off to a gentle flurry, one with big, fat, white fluffy flakes. Blue and white emergency lights flashed through the large glass front windows of the hotel. Police radios drowned out the Christmas music from the TV over the fireplace.

Malia was behind the counter, gleefully giving her statement to a detective.

A state police officer had picked up Helen Knowles and brought her to the hotel.

She came through the sliding glass doors holding a small black and white and brown beagle puppy. Later, she told me she'd forced a local shelter to open so she could adopt the dog after hearing what was in Jessie's Dear Santa letter.

Now the two of them sat at a booth talking with a couple of people. One was a female detective getting a statement from Jessie. The other was a woman from child welfare services, not the same one who'd lost Jessie in the first place. Jessie had a blanket draped over her shoulders, Teddy in the crook of her arm, and the dog sleeping on the padded seat between her and Helen, who was hugging the child like she'd never let go again.

I suspected she wouldn't. Not for a long time to come.

"All's well that ends well," the guy still calling himself Santa said, standing behind me near the fireplace.

I turned around. "We got lucky. Thanks to you. What you did up there, that took guts."

"I'm sure in your line of work, you have doubts sometimes. Doubt yourself. Doubt what it is you're doing. But don't, Grace. It's important work."

I shrugged, not sure where that was coming from. "I like to think so, but really it's just garbage collecting for a broken system."

"No, it's not." He put a hand on my shoulder. "Look at them. Look at her."

I looked over at Jessie, petting her new dog. Helen Knowles kissed the top of her head.

"Next time you get disillusioned, think about them," Santa said behind me. "Think about what would've become of her if not for you, Grace deHaviland."

His hand fell away from my shoulder.

"Wait..." I turned sharply. "I never told you my name. How'd you know...."

But the man calling himself Santa was gone.

I caught sight as the fire in the fireplace flickered erratically as if a sudden wind had blown past it. The screen over the firebox was open. Soot had spilled out onto the slate mantle.

No way.

Malia had said he was just some guy that came around every year....

I looked around. I asked everyone. No one had seen Santa leave.

Upstairs he had known Jessie's name. But I couldn't for the life of me remember telling him her name. I hadn't. I was sure of it.

I went outside and looked around, asking everyone if they'd seen him. I got the same answer. No. He was gone. He'd just vanished.

I looked to the star-filled sky. The storm clouds had moved on. The moon glowed brightly. Snow gently fell. A clear and cold and quiet night.

I half expected to hear jingle bells ringing.

No way, I told myself. It just couldn't be…

Could it?

###

If you enjoyed *Runners*, you won't want to miss

FATAL DESTINY

The first explosive full-length novel featuring
Grace deHavliand Bounty Hunter

Read on for an exciting preview…

CHAPTER ONE

GOD MUST HATE ME.

Here it was, just the second week of October, and a cold snap had moved into the area, plunging the temperatures to near freezing already. Unseasonably cold, the TV weather people said. A stalled Canadian cold front, they explained. Yeah, right. I knew what was really going on. It was God. I could hear him up in heaven, telling the angels with a laugh: *Grace deHaviland's doing surveillance. Let's make it cold as a cadaver's crotch down there.*

I cupped my hands and blew into them. Damn.

Parked in the Grandview Heights section of Columbus, I'd been sitting for hours in my beat-up cargo van in the shadows of an overhanging elm tree down the road from the only working lamp post, my full attention on a dilapidated old colonial across the street. The house was one on a block of rundown homes earmarked for demolition, something the city never seemed to get around to. In the meantime, they became havens for drug dealers, users, crack whores, and the homeless.

This one had a large front porch. The paint on the broad steps was worn to the wood, and the once-white railing had so many spindles missing it looked like a boxer's punch-drunk grin. A rusted glider was set off to one end, and an old, moldy couch sat under the large front window. The cushions on it were so worn out, they sank. Broken crack vials, fast food wrappers, and a busted tricycle littered the yard. An old box spring and rusted iron headboard leaned against the peeling siding. Junked.

I covered the light of my cell phone and checked the time: 6:30 a.m.

The darkness before the dawn.

A lone figure rounded the corner, coming from Avondale Avenue, and walking in my direction. His hands shoved in his pockets, he had his hoodie pulled up over his shaved head to ward off the chilly, pre-dawn breeze. I checked him against the mug shot I had of Tyrell Parks. It was my guy.

I opened the well-oiled van door without a sound. The dome light remained off because I'd removed the bulb months ago. The van's decrepit appearance—I'd picked it up at auction about a year ago—its dings, dents, and splotches of matte-black primer paint were deliberate, all carefully applied so no one looked twice at it. Yet mechanically, its care and maintenance was top shelf, as good as money could buy. The perfect decoy vehicle.

Jogging across the street, I avoided the splash of piss-yellow streetlight and carefully navigating my interception point. I jammed my hands into my jacket pockets, returning the mug shot of Tyrell Parks to one pocket and wrapping my hand tightly around the stun gun I carried in the other. My Colt .45 auto-loader sat snug and heavy in its holster, pressing into the small of my back. I didn't have to check for my backup piece, either. The weight of the small .32 revolver strapped to my right ankle was hard to forget.

I crossed in front of Parks, about an arm's length away, blocking his path. "Tyrell Parks."

He snapped his head up. Dark, suspicious eyes stared at me. I grabbed for his arm, but he bolted around me fast, dodging like a linebacker avoiding a tackle so that I ended up snatching air. He ran for the ramshackle old colonial.

Shit.

Up the worn steps two at a time and across the porch, he plunged through the front door, slamming it shut behind himself. Running close, two steps behind, I reached the decaying wood-and-glass door and paused, pressing my back against the clapboard frame. My heart pounded from the adrenaline surge, not the effort. I took a deep breath of

198

cold, crisp air, drew my .45, spun, and kicked in the old, weathered door.

The latch splintered inward. The door banged against the far wall with a sharp thwack and a rattle of glass. I rushed inside. Low. In the entryway, an absence of light greeted me save for the pale glow from the outside streetlamp and what little moonlight managed to leak in through the door and broken windows. Dust particles danced in the pale, ghostly hue.

I faced a center staircase. Beside it, down the left side, ran a hallway. Open archways dotted the left wall. What had once been a living room lay to my right, and opposite that, a den. Wind whistled through windows where panes were broken or missing. The walls were graffiti-tagged. Broken boards, cinderblocks, and other building debris littered the floor, and chunks of sheetrock and gravel crunched under my feet as I moved inside.

A skinny Hispanic teen stood frozen in the den, watching me. Shirtless, he had his fly open. I'd caught him urinating in the corner. He stared at me with wide, fearful eyes as his breath puffed out quick plumes of cold air.

I shoved Tyrell's mug shot into his startled face. "Where is he?"

He shook his head, muttering something I didn't catch. I jammed the picture into the pocket of my leather coat and pressed the .45 to the kid's forehead. His wide eyes grew wider. I wrinkled my nose. Ewww. He'd started peeing again.

"Where?" I repeated. "In English."

His answer came out as one long, fast word. "UpstairsIdidn'tdonothingpleasedon'thurtme."

"Gracias." I took the stairs two at a time.

At the top of the stairs, an open bathroom faced me, reeking of feces and vomit and urine. I cleared a small room to the right with a quick glance and sweep of my gun.

Down the far end of the hall, I heard a door slam.

Moving quickly, I made my way forward. Darkness filled the hallway. The air was thick with cloying dust and odors too offensive to try and identify. Open doorways stood both to my right and left. From inside came the sounds of irritated druggies rousted out of self-induced comas by the commotion. They shifted and groaned. A few shouted curses. Others remained dead to the world. Those who woke, like rats sensing danger, sat upright, listening, afraid to move and afraid not to, their addled brains racing at the speed of glaciers to make a decision. Freeze, hide, or run.

At the end of the hall, I hit the one closed door I came to with my shoulder. It gave a little then bounced back. Not locked—someone holding it.

"Tyrell Parks!" I shouted, shouldering the door again.

Pain radiated down my arm, but this time it flew open.

Inside, a soiled mattress lay on the floor. Around it was some grubby blankets, matches, candles, and other drug paraphernalia. Dull light streamed in through a busted window. Tattered, once-white lace curtains billowed from the window frame. The sash was thrown open.

Climbing out to the porch roof, Parks banged a knee on the sill and cursed.

I darted fast across the room. Crack vials and who-knew-what-else crunched under my sturdy black sneakers. I grabbed Parks by the belt…and yanked.

His hands scrambled to hold onto the sill as his baggy, oversized pants slipped down his hips, exposing even more of his purple boxers. He banged an elbow on something, cursed again, and fell back into the room. At six-one, two-hundred-twenty pounds—all of it prison yard muscle—he was built like a bull on steroids. All of that came stumbling back at me.

We hit the floor. Hard.

I grunted, worried I'd cracked a rib. Shoving him off, I gasped for air and rolled in the opposite direction. Things jabbed at me through my jacket, rusted nails, broken glass. I worried about needles. And my jacket.

It's a Piero Tucci, *damn it. If it's ruined…*

I scrambled to my feet, spun to face him, trying to control my breathing. If I appeared winded, Parks would see me as weak. I couldn't allow that. Being a woman in this business caused me enough grief as it was.

"Tyrell Parks," I said. "You're coming with me."

"Youse the cops?" On his feet, too, he faced me.

"Bail enforcement."

He cocked his head to the side like a confused puppy. "Say what?"

"Bounty hunter, asshole."

"Shit. A sista like you? No fuckin' way."

I brought up the .45, reluctant to shoot him. They don't do dead or alive anymore. Too bad—it would make things a lot easier. "No sista, bro, a hot-blooded Latina with an Irish temper. Someone you don't wanna mess with."

I planted my feet. Reading him. Afraid he might lunge.

"Sheeeet!" He charged.

A knot formed in the pit of my stomach. For an instant, I reconsidered shooting him, but I drew back my gun. I'd cold-cock the son of a bitch instead.

But he was too fast. Like lightning on crack cocaine. He swept away my arm, clamping his hand on my wrist and stopping my swing dead. He squeezed.

I gasped.

With a sharp snap of my wrist, he sent my gun flying. It landed a dozen feet away in a debris pile of studs, drywall, and pipes. With his free hand, he seized my throat and tightened his grip, lifting me off the ground. "Bitch come at me. Sheeet."

I gurgled. It was all I could do.

"Tyrell'll be learnin' you a thing 'bout manners now, bitch." He slammed me into a wall. My head bounced off the plaster. The wall shook. I saw stars, and tears filled my eyes. I'd pounded the pooch on this one, hadn't I?

He grinned, revealing a grill full of gold-capped teeth. He pressed his body into me, pinning me to the wall with all his crushing weight. Sweat and aggression radiated from him, sour and hot. And some god-awful smelling breath. So bad, I'd've gagged if I weren't being choked to death.

I thrashed around, wanting to get my loose hand inside my coat pocket. I kicked out, trying to push off the wall. Hopeless efforts.

Parks laughed at me.

I wheezed like a tire losing air.

I grew lightheaded. I was running out of oxygen and time. I tried to ignore the pain, the pressure against my chest, his smell, all of it, while I worked on getting my hand into my jacket pocket. I missed.

Fear seized me as tightly as Parks' grip.

"We's gonna have some real fun now, bitch." His face came in close to mine. I had no doubt about what he intended. Thoroughly disgusted, I turned my head. His mouth mashed wetly across my lips. His tongue raked my cheek. I vowed it wouldn't happen. I'd kill him first. Somehow.

I got my hand inside my pocket.

"Fine. No foreplay." He reached between our compressed bodies, began fumbling with his belt buckle. "We's just go right to the main event then."

"I don't think so."

My words were raspy, but I didn't care. I had the stun gun in my hand.

He got his belt unbuckled.

I jabbed the stun gun into his side. It crackled, and his body convulsed. He stumbled back, shuddering like a short-circuiting robot. I dropped to the floor—incredibly, he didn't. Though his eyes were wide and his teeth clattered like those joke dentures you see in novelty stores, he managed somehow to stay on his feet.

Angry and scared, and thinking about what almost happened to me, I charged him. A second jolt from the stun gun dropped him to his knees. Spittle drooled out of his mouth as he sputtered while his body continued to quiver. Incapacitated now, he still didn't go down.

I zapped him a third time, panting and aiming to light up his nuts. I missed, hitting his rock-hard thigh instead. Too bad, but the jolt was enough to get the job done.

His eyeballs rolled up into his head. He gurgled. Then he crashed to the floor. Down and out, but incredibly, still conscious.

Face down and twitching, he murmured something unintelligible.

I cuffed him behind his back, retrieved my .45, and, coughing, gave myself a minute to catch my breath before I hauled him up on his feet. After I did, I said, "You good to walk?"

He muttered something and nodded.

"Good." His skin was slick with sweat, and his knotted muscles still trembled. "You mess with me," I went on, "and I'll Taser you all the way down to the van. Understand?" His head lolled as if it was too heavy for his neck. I shook his arm. "Understand?"

"Yeah…yeah."

"Good."

I led him into the hall but stopped short.

A dozen shadowy figures lined the gloom of the hallway. Strung-out hopheads. Emaciated drug-zombies. They wore soiled clothes that hung off them like rags on a scarecrow. Stringy hair curtained their skull-like faces in greasy, limp ropes. Dark circles rimmed their lifeless eyes. They truly were the living dead.

"Ain't got no beef with none of y'all," I shouted. Talking street, sounding tough, I hoped. "Just Tyrell here. Don't give a rat's ass 'bout the rest of you." To me, the trash talk sounded foolish, but I kept it up as I pulled Parks along. "Y'all mess with me," I warned. "Then we throw down. You don't want that, so y'all just stay fly."

They did, and Parks and I made it downstairs and out to the street without incident. The dopers followed at a distance, gathering around the sagging porch. I yanked open the back doors of the van and pushed Parks toward it. "Get in."

I'd stripped bare the interior except for a black-iron security fence welded between the cargo space and the front seats. It was covered with a scratched-up, laminated sheet of Plexiglas. I'd been spit on enough times to have learned. Welded to the ribbed floor and along the van walls were several iron tie-down rings.

At sight, Parks hesitated. The effect of the stun gun was wearing off. I waved it in his face and squeezed the trigger. White-blue electricity crackled between the metal prongs.

"I feel you," he said, climbing in. Knowing the drill, he knelt near the rear doors. "Where's you taking me?"

"Jail." I cuffed him to a short length of chain secured to an iron ring welded into the floor.

"Ya know, bitch…." He rattled the chain for effect. "Da bruthers on them slave ships was treated better than this. Ain't no way for a sista to treat a bruther, you feel me?"

"Oh, shut up." I slammed the back doors shut.

I took Northwest Boulevard and headed downtown. Driving from the crack house, I tried to relax. But I was sore and cranky, and no amount of rolling my neck and shoulders did anything to relieve my aches or improve my mood. Excess adrenaline surged through my body, making me jittery. Fear made me shake. I tried not to think about what would have happened if I hadn't reached my stun gun in time—it had taken three zaps to put the huge bastard down. I shuddered, unable to chase the dark thoughts away.

Neither could I force away the image of those gaunt, washed-out faces I'd left behind. The drug zombies who stared at me from the front porch with their blank expressions: lost, helpless, wasted kids with nothing to live for beyond their next fix…and the sure promise of an early grave.

As I drove south on Neil, passing Nationwide Arena on my left, my cell phone rang.

The caller ID read LOUIE. The readout also read 6:53 a.m.

Large Louie Gravelle is a bail bondsman, one of several I freelance for. For Louie to be calling me at anywhere near this time of the morning could mean only one thing, and that was trouble. I flipped open the cell: "deHaviland."

Want to read on, grab *Fatal Destiny* today

To Dean and Kris

For blazing the trail and showing me the path

Once again, a shout out of thanks to my editor extraordinaire, G Miki Hayden, who worked tirelessly on each and every one of these stories, and whose expert eye and ear took what I wanted to say and made it sound so much better.

David DeLee

Thank you for purchasing this book. We hope you enjoyed it.

If you'd like to stay informed about new releases, special events, and exclusive content only available to subscribers, sign up to get David DeLee's newsletter

https://www.subscribepage.com/daviddelee

ALSO BY DAVID DELEE

Dark Justice Thrillers

Between Truth & Lies   Out of the Game
Cold Cases   With Intent
Too Far   Moral Misconduct
Stare at the Moon   Pin Money
While the City Burns   Crystal White
Takedown   Fatal Destiny
Runners

Brice Bannon Seacoast Adventures
Crimson Storm
Siege at Tiamat Bluff
The Yakuza Gambit
Strike of the Stingray
The Oceanic Princess
Facing the Storm

Parker Quinn Archaeological Thrillers
The Sudden Death

ABOUT THE AUTHOR

David DeLee is the acclaimed author behind the *Dark Justice Thrillers*, a gripping crime fiction series that brings together the bold worlds of bounty hunter Grace deHaviland, ex-DEA agent Nick Lafferty, and NYPD detectives Frank Flynn and Christine Levy. Anchored by the *Grace deHaviland Bounty Hunter* books—known for their dynamic protagonist and compelling action—DeLee's work captures the raw intensity of justice on the edge.

David also writes the high-octane *Brice Bannon Seacoast Adventure* series, a nautical action-thriller saga that captures the pulse-pounding energy of Clive Cussler, Brad Thor, and James Rollins—especially with his spin-off *Parker Quinn Archaeological Thrillers*, which blends adventure, history, and intrigue, adding a bold new layer to his ever-evolving storytelling landscape.

A former licensed private investigator and Certified Fraud Examiner with a Master's Degree in Criminal Justice, DeLee draws from real-world experience to craft authentic, edge-of-your-seat narratives that resonate with fans of crime, justice, and pulse-pounding action.

David now resides in New Hampshire, where he enjoys the lakes, the coast, and four very distinct seasons while he continues to write stories that explore the darker corners of justice.

Dark Road
PUBLISHING